GRINDING ROAD

by

Brian Bowyer

Copyright © Brian Bowyer 2024

Also by Brian Bowyer
FLESH REHEARSAL
AUTUMN GOTHIC
ALIVE UNDEAD
PERPETUAL DREAD
SINISTER MIX
APOCALYPSE
ROAD HARVEST
ROAD NARROWS
SHELF LIFE
OLD TOO SOON
KILL FACTOR
WRITING AND RISING FROM ADDICTION

Chapter 1

At the kitchen table, DeVonte drew his gun. "White boy, I should put a bullet between your eyes."

Garrett shrugged. "I know it sounds crazy, but it's true. I've repented my sins to Christ, and Jesus has forgiven me. I can no longer kill innocent children with you."

"I've seen you fuck little girls with their own femurs," DeVonte said. "You're telling me that suddenly you're a Christian?"

Garrett nodded. "That's what I'm telling you."

Thumbing the safety off, DeVonte raised his pistol and aimed it at Garrett's face. "So where does this leave us?"

"It doesn't matter. You can kill me if you want to. When I die, I know I'm going to Heaven."

"I've seen you scoop the eyes out of still-breathing kids and eat them. You somehow think you're going to Heaven?"

"For all have sinned," Garrett said, "and come short of the glory of God. But that doesn't mean I have to stop killing adults. Just no more kids. And since I know you only fuck dead women, I can still help you kill women. That won't be a problem. But if you're going to shoot me, then do it. Otherwise, Felicia needs to see us."

DeVonte lowered his gun. "Are you driving, or me?"

"You," Garrett said.

Rising from the table, DeVonte shoved his pistol into the waistband of his jeans at the small of his back.

Then Garrett got up too, and they left.

DeVonte adhered to the speed limit.

On the passenger's side, Garrett said, "Can't you drive a little faster? Felicia's pissed."

DeVonte turned the stereo down. "Man, fuck that bitch. And fuck you, too. Your white ass crashed a car into a building—drunk as hell—and got community service. If I get stopped for speeding, I might get shot in the face."

Soon thereafter, they arrived at Felicia's house. She greeted them at the front door holding a gun. Behind her stood Havoc—the biggest, blackest pit bull DeVonte had ever seen. He was not afraid of dogs, but creatures like Havoc were one of the reasons he always carried a pistol.

Felicia lowered her gun. "Garrett and DeVonte. Just the motherfuckers I wanted to see. Come on in."

She moved to the left, and they stepped inside. Felicia closed the door and locked it.

"You both owe me money," Felicia told them, in the living room.

She pointed at DeVonte. "Since you don't owe me a lot, it's not that big of a deal."

Then she turned to Garrett. "But your debt needs to be settled immediately."

DeVonte could tell that Garrett was afraid, and for good reason: Felicia—notorious as one of the most vicious crime lords in the city—was known for brutally torturing her enemies before she killed them.

While Garrett lit a cigarette, DeVonte approached the pit bull and extended a fist, which Havoc sniffed. Keeping his other hand on the gun at the small of his back, DeVonte stroked the dog's head, running his fingertips across the cropped ears, and Havoc licked his hand with a pink tongue.

"I'll get your money," Garrett told Felicia. "I just need a few more days to get it."

Felicia shook her head. "I have a better idea. Follow me."

She led them down into her basement, where they saw that she kept a naked woman strapped to a metal table. The woman was gagged, and her eyes were open. Like Garrett and Felicia, the woman was white.

"Holly?" Garrett said, staring down at the woman.

Felicia shot him a look. "You know this bitch?"

He shrugged. "I've seen her around."

From a cart beside the table, Felicia grabbed a carving knife and began removing her clothes. Soon, she was totally naked. Then she told Garrett, "This bitch owes me even more money than you do. So this is what I'm proposing: if you'll help me torture this bitch to death—and really show me that you're enjoying it—I'll knock off half the money that you owe me. What do you say?"

Garrett nodded. "You've got yourself a deal."

Felicia smiled. "Then take your clothes off. We're about to get bloody."

Garrett stripped naked, and DeVonte found the white man's penis shockingly small.

Felicia asked DeVonte, "Are you gonna join us?"

He shook his head. "I just like to watch."

"Suit yourself." She handed the knife to Garrett, then grabbed a blowtorch from the cart next to the table and turned it on.

Whimpering through her gag, Holly thrashed against the straps that secured her to the table.

Then the torture began, slow and methodical.

While Garrett and Felicia took their time destroying the woman, DeVonte pulled his penis out and stroked it. He never achieved an erection, but he did notice that Felicia kept looking at his penis and licking her lips.

Eventually, Holly died, and they all three walked back upstairs. DeVonte was the only one with clothes on. Garrett and Felicia stood naked and covered in blood.

Felicia looked at Garrett, and smiled. "I've changed my mind."

Then she whistled for Havoc, and the pit bull entered the living room. "Havoc," Felicia said, pointing at Garrett, "sic."

Instantly, the pit bull attacked the white man.

DeVonte watched the dog hit Garrett in the chest with his forepaws, sending him to the floor on his back. Then Havoc clamped his jaws around Garrett's neck and chewed his throat open. Arterial blood shot out in a crimson abundance.

As Garrett bled to death, DeVonte reached into his jeans and began stroking his erection.

"I can help you with that," Felicia told him. "Wanna join me in the shower?"

He nodded. "Do you have any beer?"

"In the fridge. Grab two. I'll be in the shower, getting ready for you." She left the room and took off down the hall.

Moments later, DeVonte heard water falling from the shower in the bathroom.

He drew his gun from the small of his back, attached a sound suppressor to its threaded barrel, and whistled for Havoc. The pit bull turned around.

DeVonte shot the dog through the head, killing him instantly. Then he found a butcher's knife in the kitchen and took it into the bathroom.

In the shower, Felicia sang beneath the falling water.

Raising the knife, DeVonte yanked the shower curtain aside. "I only fuck dead women," he told her.

Felicia screamed.

Chapter 2

Tina opened her eyes. Chomping and slurping noises had woken her up. Raising her head, she saw Victor on the floor next to the bed, chewing on the femur of the girl she murdered last night. The Rottweiler had stripped most of the flesh from the dead girl's leg.

I'll clean the blood up later, Tina thought.

She got up, brushed her teeth, and took a shower. Then she put some clothes on and went downstairs.

In the living room, Leo sat on the sofa, cleaning a disassembled pistol. In the shoulder rig he wore, the grip of another pistol was visible.

Jinx sat on the loveseat, reading an old copy of *Interview with the Vampire.*

"I didn't know black dudes liked to read romance novels," Tina told him.

Looking up from the book, Jinx cocked his head. "Anne Rice wasn't a romance novelist."

Tina rolled her eyes. "Whatever."

Jinx asked Leo, "What do you think, white boy? Was Anne Rice a romance novelist, or a horror novelist?"

Leo shrugged. "I have no idea." Then he looked at Tina. "Speaking of romance, where's that girl you brought home from the club last night?"

"She's upstairs, but she's dead. I had to kill her."

Leo shook his head. "Crazy bitch."

"I'm not crazy," Tina said. "She freaked out and became a completely different person after she got here."

Closing his book, Jinx asked her, "Why are you cheating on Roxanne, anyway?"

Tina shot him a look. "What are you talking about?"

"Well, if you're in a relationship with Roxanne, you shouldn't be hooking up with other girls."

"It's not a monogamous relationship," Tina said. "She and I have agreed to see other people. And Roxanne says she's too old for me, anyway."

"Yeah," Jinx said. "You are pretty young. You're not even twenty-one yet, are you?"

"Nope. Still twenty."

"And how old's Roxanne?"

"Thirty-four."

Jinx nodded. "Yep. Quite a bit older than you, but thirty-four's still young for a best-selling author. And she still looks mighty fine at thirty-four. Does she only date women?"

"No. Roxanne dates men, too."

"What about black men? Does she date black men?"

Tina shrugged. "I don't know. Why wouldn't she?"

"I don't know," Jinx said. "Some white chicks won't date black dudes."

"That's weird."

Tina sat down on the sofa next to Leo, who continued cleaning his disassembled pistol. A bottle of whiskey stood on the coffee table, and she took a drink.

Then she told Jinx, "Roxanne's out of town, but maybe you can hook up with her when she gets back."

"What's she doing out of town?"

"She's out on the road, doing a book-signing tour."

"That sounds fun," Jinx said. "You should have gone with her."

Tina nodded. "I wanted to, but she wouldn't let me. She told me she's too dangerous."

"Too dangerous?"

"Yeah. She told me there's a lot about her that I don't know."

Jinx laughed. "She's a fucking writer. She just *writes* about crazy shit. Does she have any idea how fucking crazy you are? She's a horror novelist. You're a schizophrenic, homicidal maniac."

Tina lit a cigarette. "I'm not that bad when I'm on my medication."

"Yeah, but you never take the shit."

"Still, it's a valid excuse. What's your excuse? You two kidnap people and take them to Washington, D.C. to be eaten by cannibal politicians."

"Slow down," Jinx said. "That doesn't mean we're crazy. Those politicians pay us well to bring them human meat."

Leo took a drink. "Besides, if we didn't do it, someone else would."

Tina shrugged. "I suppose." Rising from the sofa, she told them, "Don't worry about that corpse in my bedroom. I'll deal with it later."

She headed toward the door.

"Do you need a ride somewhere?" Leo asked her.

"Nope. I'm just gonna go walk around the city for a while. See what sort of mischief I can get into."

"L.A.'s a big city," Jinx told her. "I hope you don't get lost."

Tina smiled. "We'll see."

She left.

Chapter 3

During a flight back to Los Angeles from Seattle, Roxanne Hargrove sat reading a novel in business class. The man next to her nudged her with an elbow.

"Last night," he said, looking down at his phone, "coyotes killed two newlyweds in California while they were camping on their honeymoon."

Roxanne did not reply.

"Also last night," the man went on, "cougars attacked and killed two hikers camping in Montana."

"Is that so?"

"Yes. This morning, a grizzly bear killed a fisherman in British Columbia, a pack of wolves killed a toddler in Wisconsin, and a mountain lion killed a climber in Colorado."

Roxanne closed her book. "Why are you telling me this?"

"Because the animals are running out of room, and their attacks on humans are a result of humanity's encroachment on their territory. Experts predict that within the next ten years, even more unspoiled land on this planet—totaling an area larger than North America—will be damaged by human activity, which means that more than eighty percent of Earth's land surface will either be disturbed, fragmented, or destroyed by roads, cities, and other infrastructure of human civilization. So it's no surprise that the animals—predators and prey alike—are wandering into more and more people's back yards every night. These casualties we've been seeing are inevitable, and will only get worse."

Roxanne cast her gaze through the window to her left: dark clouds in the moonlight beyond the glass.

"This afternoon," the man continued, "marsupial lions attacked a group of kindergartners in Sydney, Australia, killing four children on a playground."

Roxanne shot him a look. "Marsupial lions have been extinct for thirty thousand years."

The man shook his head. "That's a myth. Marsupial lions are still alive."

Roxanne opened her book. "If you say so."

"You look familiar, by the way. I'm Tim Carter. What's your name?"

"Roxanne. Last name's Hargrove."

"Roxanne Hargrove? The novelist?"

She nodded. "That's me."

He laughed. "Small world! My wife's a fan of your work. I don't read fiction, but she reads all your books. Mind if I take a selfie with you in it?"

"Yes, I *do* mind, actually. No offense."

"None taken," he said, but she could tell he was displeased.

Roxanne paid him no mind the rest of the flight.

***

Elmore Hollister was in a fabulous mood. After spending the weekend with his mistress in Orange County, he drove back to West Hollywood with the top down. The night wind felt wonderful in his hair, and his Ferrari handled the highway like a dream. His flask of whiskey lay next to him on the passenger's seat, but he wasn't worried about getting a DUI. He was a celebrity now, an Oscar-winning director, and he always carried plenty of cash in his wallet with which to bribe the police.

His house was built split-level into a hillside. He parked in the garage, fetched his whiskey, and rode an elevator up to the second floor.

The interior was quiet. His wife probably lay unconscious upstairs under the influence of sedatives and alcohol. He turned a TV on for noise, then went into the kitchen, where he finished the whiskey in his flask. Then he grabbed a bottle of whiskey from the cupboard and walked up to the third floor.

Shock took his breath away as soon as he entered the master bedroom. His wife's severed head sat between two pillows, propped upright on its neck stump. The lips had been removed, exposing teeth. The open eyes were rolled back in their sockets. Her torso lay before the head atop the mattress, surrounded by her four severed limbs. He saw blood, internal organs, and chunks of flesh everywhere. The slaughterhouse stench was overpowering.

Elmore had married this woman ten years ago, when he was an unknown filmmaker, and had—since his success—often fantasized about divorce. But now, seeing her like this, butchered and dissected, he felt a love for her as strong as any since their honeymoon in Vegas. *She didn't deserve this,* he thought. *Jesus. No one does. It doesn't make sense.*

He vomited on the floor and started weeping.

"Good evening, director."

A female voice, behind him.

He spun around, and it took a few seconds to process what he saw: Roxanne Hargrove, the author of a book he had recently made into a movie, naked and covered in blood, pointing what looked like a toy gun at his chest from six feet away.

"Why?" he said. "For the love of God, why? You told me you *liked* the film! You told me you *enjoyed* the adaptation!"

Roxanne cocked her head. "I did, but this has nothing to do with that. Sometimes, I just like to kill."

Then pain blasted though his body. Elmore felt his muscles freeze before he hit the floor. He never lost consciousness, however. Looking down, he saw two conductive wires attached to probes embedded in his chest.

That wasn't a toy gun, he thought. *That was a taser.*

***

Hours later, after torturing, killing, and dismembering the director, Roxanne left to catch a flight to Nashville.

Chapter 4

After killing Felicia, DeVonte fucked her corpse in the shower. While scrubbing her blood from his body beneath the falling water, he thought, *Now I have to leave San Francisco.*

Before he left, he found some cash in her bedroom and put it in his pocket. *There's probably more around here somewhere,* he thought, *but I ain't got time to search the house.*

Felicia had been a well-connected crime boss, and if the wrong person found out he had killed her, he knew he would be just as dead as she was.

Forty-five minutes later, using a pay phone in San Jose, DeVonte called his brother in Los Angeles.

Chapter 5

While Jinx sat reading on the loveseat, Leo rose from the sofa and said, "Have you seen Victor this evening?"

Not looking up from his book, Jinx shook his head. "Nope. He's probably upstairs in Tina's room."

Leo walked upstairs to the second floor of the compound's main house.

In Tina's room, he found Victor on the floor at the foot of her bed, chewing on the femur of the girl she had murdered last night. The rest of the girl's carcass lay scattered throughout the room, but the floor was hardwood, so it wasn't that big of a deal. Besides, Tina already told them she would clean up the mess when she got home.

"Are you hungry, Victor?" Leo said.

Cocking his massive head, the Rottweiler stopped gnawing on the femur and looked up at him.

"I'm gonna go grab some food," Leo said, "so I'll bring you something to eat when I get home."

Victor resumed chewing on the bone.

Leo turned and headed back downstairs.

In the living room, he put a jacket on to conceal his shoulder rig. Then he asked Jinx, "Are you hungry?"

Still reading, Jinx shrugged. "I don't know. I guess."

"I'm gonna go grab some food. You wanna ride with me?"

Jinx shot him a look. "White boy, you've been drinking since noon. How about I drive you instead?"

Leo grabbed his bottle from the coffee table and took a drink. "That's cool. Whatever you wanna do."

Jinx closed his book and set it on the coffee table. His shoulder rig lay on the floor, next to the loveseat. He strapped it on and shoved his pistol into the holster beneath his left arm. Then he rose from the loveseat and put his jacket on. "Let me hit that whiskey. I need to catch up with your drunk ass."

Leo laughed. "I'm not drunk." He handed Jinx the bottle.

Jinx took a drink and set the bottle down.

They left.

Leo closed the door behind them. "Think I should lock it? Do you think Tina remembered to take her key?"

"No idea, but she'd probably forget her head if it wasn't attached to her shoulders, so just leave it unlocked. Ain't nobody coming in our house, anyway."

"That's true," Leo said. "And even if they do, Victor will make them wish they goddamn hadn't."

While crossing the lawn, Leo glanced over at the barn in which their tour bus was parked, knowing that soon he and Jinx would have to start filling the bus with humans while traveling east to the cannibals in Washington, D.C. *Those politicians are due for another feast,* he thought. *Senator Fox will call us soon and tell us to hit the road . . .*

"Toss me the keys," Jinx told him, when they reached the Cadillac.

Leo tossed him the keys, and they got in. Jinx started the engine. Leo cracked his window on the passenger's side.

Fifteen minutes later, they stopped at a fast-food restaurant.

At the drive-through window, as they waited for their order (burgers and fries for themselves; a bucket of fried chicken for Victor), Jinx's phone rang.

Leo turned the stereo off. "That might be Senator Fox."

Withdrawing the phone from his pocket, Jinx checked its screen. "Nope, it's not Fox. It's Pops."

Leo said, "That means he has a job for us."

Pops—an old crime boss they had known for many years—still ran a nightclub in downtown L.A. at seventy years of age. They supplemented their income by working for Pops when they weren't abducting humans for the government.

Jinx answered the call, spoke for only a few seconds, then disconnected.

"Well?" Leo said. "Was I right?"

Jinx nodded. "He wants us in his office as soon as possible."

After they got their food, they went straight to The Way Down Lounge. Leaving the food in the car, they got out and went inside.

The place was packed. A live band played rock music on a stage to the left.

At the bar, Jinx told the bartender, "We're here to see Pops."

The bartender nodded. "He's downstairs in his office, expecting you. I'll let him know you're here."

Leo followed Jinx to a door in the back of the club, which opened onto a staircase, and they descended.

At the end of a hallway, Jinx knocked on the door of Pops's office, then opened it. "Hello, Pops. We got here as fast as we could."

Pops, seated behind his desk, removed his glasses and set them down. "Yes, I see this. Come on in."

They stepped into his office.

"Have a seat."

Each sat down on one of the two chairs across from Pops's desk.

"I'll keep this brief," he said. "I need you to kill a doctor here in Los Angeles."

Leo cocked his head. "A doctor?"

"Yes, a surgeon. And the family that's paying me wants you to videotape the whole thing." He opened a drawer, withdrew an old-fashioned VHS camcorder, and set it on his desk.

"Jesus Christ," Leo said. "I didn't even think they made those things anymore."

Pops shrugged. "I think it's refurbished."

Jinx said, "Does it even work?"

"Of course it works. And there's a blank tape already in it." From his shirt's breast pocket, Pops withdrew a folded sheet of paper and handed it to Jinx. "Now listen: the family that's paying me wants you to torture the doctor before you kill him, and they have some specific requests. The details are on that sheet of paper. After you read it, burn it."

Jinx nodded, shoving the piece of paper into his pocket. "You got it."

Pops then handed them each a thick envelope. "Here's the first half of your money. After you kill the doctor, bring me the tape and I'll pay you the other half."

"Sounds good," Jinx said, rising from his chair.

Leo got up too and grabbed the camcorder.

"Think you can figure out how to use that thing?" Pops asked him.

Leo shrugged. "Shouldn't be too difficult, but if they want us to film the torture scenes, we're gonna have to get some masks."

"Yes," Pops told them. "That's not a bad idea."

They left.

In the car, before Jinx started the engine, his phone rang again, and he checked its screen.

"Senator Fox?" Leo asked him.

"Nope. I have no idea who this is."

Jinx answered the phone, spoke briefly, and then disconnected. "That was my brother," he said. "He needs a place to lay low for a few days, so I told him he could stay at our place."

Leo nodded. "Cool. So he lives here in L.A.?"

"No. He's on his way down here right now from San Francisco."

"What's his name?"

Jinx started the engine. "DeVonte, and he's a crazy motherfucker."

"Then he'll fit right in with the rest of us," Leo said.

Jinx put the car on the road, and they headed back to the compound.

Chapter 6

"Do you come here often?" the young man asked Tina, in the club. He sat on the stool to her left at the bar.

Tina sipped her drink. "No. It's my first time here."

"Oh yeah?"

"Yes. I'm not even from L.A."

"Really? Where are you from?"

"Virginia."

"Wow. You're a long way from home. What brings you to L.A.?"

"It's a long story."

"Did you wanna be an actress, or something?"

"No. Let's just say I was in a bad situation, and two guys got me out of the bad situation, and now I live with those guys here in L.A."

"So you live with two guys?"

"Yes, but it's not what you're thinking. I don't fuck guys, anyway. I only fuck chicks."

The young man shrugged. "That's cool."

"But if I *did* fuck guys," Tina said, "I would definitely consider fucking you. You're definitely hot."

"You think so?"

"Yes. What are you? A rock star, or something?"

Smiling, he shook his head. "No, but I *am* a musician."

She nodded. "I thought so."

"I'm Carter, by the way."

"I'm Tina, and I'm looking for some heroin."

Carter laughed.

"What's so funny?"

"Nothing," he said. "But you're in luck, because I happen to have some heroin back at my place."

"Is that right?"

"Yes. My house is only a few blocks away. You wanna go do some?"

Tina cocked her head. "How do I know you're not a serial killer?"

Carter laughed again. "Listen, I'm not a serial killer, I assure you. The truth is, I don't like hanging out with other guys. I much prefer hanging out with girls. And since you don't fuck guys anyway, that takes all the pressure of sex out of the situation, and we can just relax, hang out, and have fun. So, what do you say? You wanna go shoot some heroin?"

Tina finished her drink. "I walked here. Can I ride with you?"

"Of course."

They left, and he drove her to his house a few blocks away.

"Nice place," Tina said, after they stepped into the living room.

Carter gestured toward the sofa. "Have a seat."

Tina sat down, and Carter left the room, returning moments later holding a tray. He joined her on the sofa and set the tray on the coffee table. On the tray were two spoons, a glass of water, a box of Q-tips, a cigarette lighter, and two hypodermic syringes with needles attached.

From a compartment beneath the tabletop, Carter produced a small bag of white powder. He dumped some of the powder out and split it up into two hits.

"Is that some good heroin?" Tina asked him.

He nodded. "It sure is."

Tina watched him draw water from the glass with a syringe and press it out into one of the spoons. He stirred one of the hits up with the water in the spoon and cooked it over a flame from the cigarette lighter. He cooked the heroin until it hissed, put the lighter down, and drew the hit from the spoon into the syringe. Then he flicked air out of the syringe and handed it to Tina. "All yours," Carter said.

The needle looked clean to Tina, but she sterilized it with the cigarette lighter anyway. Then she found a vein and injected herself. Euphoria was instantaneous, and a pleasant warmth spread throughout her body. She leaned back on the sofa, watching Carter prepare the other dose, and then he injected himself, too.

Soon thereafter, Carter said, "I'm not a serial killer, but I *could* be suicidal, and maybe I wanna take you out with me. For all you know, I put some fentanyl in the heroin, and we could both be dead in a matter of seconds."

Tina shrugged. "I don't give a fuck. I'm not scared of death."

"You're not?"

"Hell, no. Besides, if you were suicidal, you could have killed us both in your car, on the way over here, with one wrong turn of the steering wheel."

"I suppose that's true," Carter said. "But I'm not suicidal . . . *most* of the time."

Tina shot him a look. "So sometimes you're suicidal?"

"Yeah, sometimes. But not right now."

Tina nodded. "That's cool. Sometimes I'm suicidal, too."

They sat in silence momentarily, then Carter said, "So how would you do it, anyway? How would you commit suicide?"

"I'd jump off a skyscraper," Tina said.

"Really?"

"Yes. I mean, you can cut your wrists, or take a bottle of pills, or try to hang yourself, or shoot yourself, or what have you, but none of those are foolproof. If you jump off a tall building, however, you're not gonna survive that shit."

"Some people do," Carter said.

Tina shook her head. "Then the building wasn't tall enough."

Carter nodded. "You're probably right. And they probably did it wrong, anyway. You should definitely try to hit the ground headfirst."

It was then she saw a bedbug emerge from Carter's hair and crawl down the side of his face. She sprang up from the sofa. "JESUS FUCKING CHRIST! YOU BROUGHT ME HERE KNOWING YOU HAVE A BEDBUG INFESTATION?"

Carter cocked his head. "What are you talking about?"

Tina looked down: she saw bedbugs crawling up her pants and across her shoes. "SON OF A BITCH!"

Carter said, "What the hell is wrong with you?"

From her back pocket, Tina withdrew the folding knife she carried. "BEDBUGS, YOU BASTARD! I'LL HAVE TO BURN MY CLOTHES! I'LL HAVE TO CUT MY HAIR AND SHAVE MY HEAD!" She flicked open the knife.

"Have you lost your mind?" Carter said, rising from the sofa. "There are no bedbugs here."

Grabbing a fistful of her own hair, Tina raised the folding knife. Then she turned to face Carter and blacked out . . .

***

She came to in the living room, holding the knife. Carter lay butchered on the floor. His gory remains were splattered all over the walls, the floor, the sofa, the TV—even the ceiling.

But she didn't see any bedbugs anywhere.

Did I hallucinate the bedbugs? Tina wondered.

No, she thought. *The bedbugs had been real. They had simply returned to their hiding places, where they wait until you're asleep before emerging to suck your blood like an army of vampires.*

She thought about taking a shower in Carter's bathroom, but decided against it. Instead, Tina fled.

Covered in blood, she kept to the shadows as she ran.

Chapter 7

Cecelia Parcell, at twenty-four, had—according to music critics—worked long and hard to get so far so soon. But what those critics failed to mention was the fact that she would have been in Nashville much sooner, perhaps as early as eighteen years of age, pursuing her dream of country-music stardom, had her mother not been stricken with leukemia.

Cecelia, an only child, had been singing for as long as she could remember. Born in Canada, in a rural part of Ontario, she lost her father in a fishing accident when she was four. He had kept an acoustic guitar in the house, and she began playing around with it after he died. Playing guitar came naturally to Cecelia, but her voice was what had truly amazed her mother. After Athina heard her daughter sing, she told Cecelia she had been born with perfect pitch.

Her father's life insurance was minimal, and his death left them destitute. Athina took jobs in various mills and factories to ensure their survival. She worked hard, and her daughter was never denied basic necessities or education. And at night, with work and school behind them, young Cecelia filled their home with music.

Athina never remarried, and their lives were loving and simple until the leukemia came along and changed everything.

The leukemia—chronic—began in Athina's bone marrow, and Cecelia dropped out of high school to support them. Canada provided free health care for its citizens, but someone had to feed them and keep the lights on.

Her mother fought a long, resilient battle, but the disease finally claimed her at age forty-three. She died in her own bed, with her daughter by her side.

The end came on a full-moon night. In the moments following death's visitation, Cecelia clutched her mother's hands and wept. She then called emergency services to report her mother's death. While waiting for someone to arrive, she fetched her father's guitar and wrote a song.

After the burial, Cecelia sold the house and moved to Tennessee.

***

In Nashville, Roxanne got in the back of a taxi in front of a hotel on Nolensville Road.

"Where to?" the driver said.

"Downtown."

The driver put the taxi on the road. He apparently itched all over, scratching himself the whole time he drove.

"I'm Benicio," he said. "You wouldn't happen to have any pills, would you?"

"Pills?"

"Yes. I'm going through withdrawal, and need something to take the edge off."

Roxanne gave him one of the Xanax pills her psychiatrist prescribed for anxiety.

"Thank you," he said. "And you don't owe me anything for the ride."

Soon thereafter, she stepped out of the cab at the intersection of Broadway and Music Row.

***

Backstage in the club, Cecelia sat before a mirror, sipping her fourth vodka tonic before the show. While putting her makeup on, she applied the highlights lightly, so they wouldn't smear beneath the spotlight. She wore her blond hair in a ponytail, but curled ropes had escaped to frame her face.

Twenty-four years old, she thought, *and I see more lines every day.*

Her beauty would fade, she knew, and eventually, so too would her voice.

But not tonight . . .

Cecelia finished her drink. Then she grabbed her father's guitar and headed toward the stage.

***

Roxanne walked the downtown streets of Nashville, dressed in black. The night was warm, devoid of wind. Street musicians performed on every corner. Youngsters swept by on skateboards and rollerblades. Couples walked around smiling and holding hands.

Prostitutes leaned against lampposts, but Roxanne wanted to kill more than a prostitute tonight—and she already had a victim selected. At ten p.m., she walked into the crowded club on Eighth Avenue where Cecelia Parcell was performing.

Roxanne was not a fan of country music, but Cecelia's voice was one of the best she had ever heard. After watching her video for a song called "Mama's Girl" online, she could hardly believe Cecelia was not already a superstar.

Approaching the stage, Roxanne stopped to watch her perform from four rows back. The crowd loved her, and yet Cecelia never smiled, not even when the audience applauded.

Clutching her purse, Roxanne pondered which of the knives it contained she would use on Cecelia first.

***

Cecelia was drunk. She had been drinking vodka the entire show, and her final set concluded at two a.m. She finished her show with the song she had written in her mother's bedroom after she died.

When "Mama's Song" ended, she saw a few women crying in the front row. Four rows back, a woman in black wiped tears from her eyes with a tissue, and waved.

Cecelia waved back. Then she put her dead father's guitar in its case and left the stage.

***

Roxanne watched Cecelia drink at the bar until closing time, then followed her outside into the night. She let Cecelia stagger ahead of her a few paces, then closed the distance between them and said, "Excuse me."

Cecelia turned around. "Oh," she said, smiling. "I remember you. What can I do for you, beautiful?" Her speech was slurred, and she reeked of alcohol. Her eyes were bloodshot.

"You're staggering," Roxanne said, "and I'm afraid you're gonna fall. Let me carry your guitar to your car for you."

Cecelia laughed. "Thanks!" She handed Roxanne the case. "Daddy's guitar," she said. "I was always a mama's girl, but I've been playin' Daddy's guitar my entire life." She swayed on her feet, but didn't fall. "And I don't drive a car. I drive a truck."

"Where is your truck parked?" Roxanne said.

Cecelia spun around and pointed at a blue, newer-model truck. "Right over there."

"You should let me drive you home. You're in no condition to drive."

"You can drive me home anytime," Cecelia said.

Roxanne smiled. "I'm glad to hear that."

She kept Cecelia from falling while helping her to the truck, which had an extended cab, and Roxanne put the guitar behind the front seats.

They got in. Cecelia gave her the keys, and Roxanne started the engine. Then Cecelia guided her to a small house near Vanderbilt University.

They got out and went inside.

"Nice place," Roxanne said, pulling the taser from her purse.

"Thanks! Can I get you something to drink?"

Roxanne zapped her with the taser, and Cecelia went down. Then Roxanne choked her unconscious and dragged her into a bedroom.

***

Cecelia opened her eyes with a headache, sitting on a chair. She tried to get up, but could not. Then she realized she was not merely sitting on the chair—she was tied to it. Even worse, she was *naked* and tied to the chair. Ropes bound her chest and waist, and more ropes were tied across her thighs, securing her to the seat. Her arms were fastened to the arms of the chair below her elbows, and again at her wrists. The chair was one of her kitchen chairs that someone had moved into her bedroom.

What the fuck?

In addition to having a headache, Cecelia was also still intoxicated. The last thing she remembered was talking to the woman who had driven her home—then blackness.

As if on cue, the woman entered the bedroom, totally naked. She held a carving knife in one hand and pliers in the other. A large purse dangled from her neck. "I'm glad you're awake," she said. "You and I are about to have some fun."

Setting the knife and the pliers on the floor, she withdrew a ball-gag from her purse, shoved its rubber sphere into Cecelia's mouth, and strapped its leather harness around her head. "All those scars that cover your body . . . were they self-inflicted?"

Cecelia nodded, noticing that the woman's body, too, was covered in scars.

"I thought so. Most of my scars were self-inflicted, too. Some would say the way we mutilate ourselves is unreasonable, that it's absurd to inflict physical pain upon ourselves as a way of relieving emotional pain, but at least the physical pain is a pain that we can locate—and a pain that can therefore be relieved. The emotional pain is worse. We hurt everywhere, at all times, and there's no way the pain can be relieved."

Setting her purse on the floor, the woman picked up the pliers and the carving knife. "Tonight, all your emotional pain comes to an end."

Numerous things flashed through Cecelia's mind: photographs of her father, and his guitar that she still played; her mother's disease and terrible death back home in Canada; her gift of music and moving to Nashville to chase her dreams.

Unable to speak, Cecelia looked into the woman's eyes. *So this is it? This was my destiny all along? For my life to end this way?*

"You were born to sing," the woman said. "And I was born to kill and tell stories."

She raised the knife. "Tonight, while I torture you to death, I'm gonna tell you about my recurring dream."

Cecelia closed her eyes, but the woman forced them open.

***

In Roxanne's dream, she's three years old again, standing before a cake with three burning candles in its center. Her chin barely crests the kitchen table. Her mother stands beside her, and Roxanne looks up at her.

"Go ahead, Roxanne! Make a wish!"

She blows out all three candles and the dream shifts to when she's four years old, playing with a plastic shovel and a plastic bucket in her sandbox. Her mother is on her knees across the yard, planting seeds in her flowerbed. The day is warm. The grass is green. Birds sing beneath a yellow sun.

The dream shifts. Her mother sits on the living-room sofa, crying.

"What's wrong, Mommy?"

"Your daddy died serving his country."

Roxanne doesn't remember her father, but there's a photograph of the man on top of the television. Someone on the TV screen is talking about a war.

The dream shifts. Roxanne is six years old now, growing up to be a fine little lady, is what her mommy says. She's doing well with her studies in first grade at elementary school. She has a new daddy now. He works in the coal mines, and comes home every night covered in coal dust. Roxanne can tell he doesn't like her. He never talks unless he's shouting, and he never has anything nice to say. He reads his bible a lot, and often slaps her mother in the face.

The dream shifts to summertime, and school shuts down for the season. Her mother says it's the driest July in living memory, and she only keeps her flowers alive by watering them. The heat is a constant, evil presence. Her mother keeps the windows open, and they fan each other with newspapers. New Daddy comes home from work every night in a terrible mood. He punches holes in the walls, and slaps her mother when she doesn't do what he says. When he's home on weekends, Roxanne stays in her room as much as possible.

But sometimes, late at night, when her mother is asleep, New Daddy enters Roxanne's room with a butcher's knife. He pulls away her blanket and tosses it aside. "Take your clothes off, girl, or I'll shove this goddamn knife into your eyes." Roxanne's hands go up reflexively, and New Daddy rolls her over and takes her pajamas off.

The dream shifts. Four years have passed. Roxanne is now ten years old. She steps out of the school bus into a rainstorm and dashes into the trailer. Her mother clips coupons from a newspaper with scissors at the kitchen table. Lightning flashes, thunder ensues, and then something begins pounding the roof.

"It's hail!" her mother says. "My flowers are going to die!" She hurries outside into the storm with her metal scissors.

Roxanne follows her out, but stops on the covered porch. Ice falls from the sky and pummels everything. Her mother is halfway to the flowerbed when an arc of lightning strikes her and takes her away, leaving nothing behind but a pair of slippers.

The dream shifts. She's in a cemetery. New Daddy stands next to her at Mommy's burial. A shoebox is lowered into the earth. Roxanne tosses flowers into the grave, then dirt is shoveled into the hole.

The dream shifts. New Daddy enters Roxanne's bedroom. Tonight, just like every night since Mommy got taken away on a bolt of lightning, New Daddy raises a knife and strips her naked.

The dream shifts. A teacher notices Roxanne's bruises and calls the police. New Daddy gets arrested, and Roxanne gets taken from the trailer.

The dream shifts. Nothing has prepared her for the horrors of the orphanage . . .

***

By the time Roxanne stopped talking, Cecelia's remains lay scattered all over the bedroom.

She took a shower in the adjoining bathroom. Then she drove Cecelia's truck to within walking distance of her hotel and abandoned it.

Later that morning, during a flight back to Los Angeles, Roxanne closed her eyes and took a nap. She didn't dream.

Chapter 8

The sun had not yet set when DeVonte arrived in Los Angeles. Just east of downtown, he drove to the address his brother had given him over the phone, which turned out to be a compound on a hill overlooking a cemetery. At the top of the hill, he parked in front of the main house and got out. *This place is huge,* DeVonte thought, looking around at the cabins, barns, and other buildings.

Then some white girl and a Rottweiler stepped out of the main house and approached him. "Who the fuck are you?" the white girl said.

He detected no hostility in her question—only genuine curiosity. "I'm DeVonte," he said, staring at the Rottweiler. "I'm Jinx's brother. Is that dog friendly?"

"He is if I tell him to be. His name is Victor. And yeah, Jinx told me that he had a brother who was coming to stay with us. I'm Tina, by the way. It's nice to meet you."

"It's nice to meet you, too." DeVonte swept his gaze across the property. "This place looks like the set of an old movie."

Tina laughed. "That's what I thought, when I first got here. Then Leo told me that people *did* used to make movies here, a long time ago."

"Is Leo the white dude who lives here with Jinx?"

"Yep. Have you met him?"

"No, I haven't. Jinx told me that he lived here with some white dude, but he never mentioned his name. He didn't tell me that a white girl lived here, too."

"I'm still new here," Tina said, rubbing Victor's head. "Well, *kinda* new, anyway. Jinx and Leo picked me up in Virginia."

"Virginia?"

"Yeah. They rescued me, actually, more so than picked me up. It's a long story. Anyway, they're not home right now, but you can just grab your stuff and come on in." She turned and headed back toward the main house, and the Rottweiler followed her.

DeVonte grabbed his suitcase from the car and followed them inside.

"Nice place," he said, in the living room, which was clean. Shelves filled with books lined the walls, and he saw a bottle of whiskey on the coffee table.

Victor plopped down on the floor and started gnawing on a rawhide bone.

Tina asked DeVonte, "Are you hungry? There's plenty of canned foods in the kitchen, and we have a lot of frozen foods, too."

DeVonte shook his head. "Not right now. Maybe later."

She pointed to a staircase. "There's an empty bedroom on the second floor, next to my room, so you can have that. It's the last door on the left. And you'll have your own bathroom, too."

"Cool." DeVonte took his suitcase upstairs.

When he came back down, Tina sat on the sofa, drinking whiskey. "Mind if I join you?" he asked her.

Tina shook her head. "Be my guest."

DeVonte sat down next to her on the sofa. "Damn," he said, looking at her bottle. "You're drinking that cowboy-killer shit."

"Cowboy-killer shit?"

"Yeah. Whiskey's the shit that killed the cowboys."

"Your brother drinks whiskey. Are you calling Jinx a cowboy?"

"No, I ain't calling him anything, but maybe he's been hanging out with you white folks too much."

Tina shot him a look. "You got something against white folks?"

"Nah, it's cool. I ain't got nothing against white folks. The truth is, I don't like anybody."

Tina took a drink. "Same here, pretty much. Well, except for hot chicks. I *love* hot chicks. What about you? Do you like hot chicks?"

"Nope. I prefer them cold."

"Cold?"

"Yep. No warmer than room temperature."

Tina cocked her head. Then she cracked a grin. "Dude, you're a freak."

DeVonte smiled. "You have no idea. Let me hit that whiskey."

She handed him the bottle. He took a drink and gave the bottle back.

Tina turned the TV on, flipped to a nature program, and set the remote back down.

"You should tell me that story you mentioned earlier," DeVonte said.

"Story?"

"Yeah, about my brother and the white dude rescuing you."

"Ah, okay. Well, what happened was . . . I was seeing a shrink in Virginia—"

"A shrink?"

"Yeah, a psychiatrist."

"What the fuck were you seeing a shrink for?"

"To get meds, mainly. I'm bipolar and schizophrenic, but it turned out the doctor was even crazier than I am. He killed my parents, abducted me, and kept me prisoner in his basement."

"Kept you prisoner?"

"Yeah. He tied me with rope to an old radiator."

"Damn."

"I know, right? Anyway, Jinx and Leo showed up at his place to buy some drugs on their way to Washington, D.C., and they heard me yelling down in the basement. They ended up killing the doctor, but it had nothing to do with me. They were just robbing him, I guess. Then they came down to see who was making all the noise in the basement, and found me."

"I'm surprised they didn't kill you, too," DeVonte said.

Tina took a drink. "I guess they had pity on me, or some shit, because they cut me loose and told me I was free to go. The only problem was, I *had* nowhere to go, so I asked them if I could go with them, and they said yes. Then we all three took off in their tour bus."

"Tour bus?"

"Yes." She pointed to the Rottweiler. "It's where I first met Victor. He was inside the bus, guarding the hostages. Or captives. Whatever you wanna call them."

DeVonte cocked his head. "What are you talking about?"

"I'm talking about human fucking livestock. They had people handcuffed to poles inside the bus, and they had human corpses in a meat freezer, too."

"Seriously?"

"Yep. They had snatched the people from the highways while traveling east. When we got to Washington, D.C., they delivered the people to cannibal politicians in a warehouse downtown."

"Cannibal politicians?"

Tina nodded. "I shit you not. The politicians were having a dinner party inside the warehouse, and the humans were the main fucking course. But the warehouse only looked like a warehouse from the outside. Once you got inside, it looked like a ballroom, with men in white tuxedos and women in white dresses and ball gowns. The whole thing was crazy."

"I'll be damned," DeVonte said. "Jinx told me a while back that he was working for the U.S. government, but he didn't go into details. Is that where he's at right now? Are he and the white dude out on the road in the tour bus, abducting people for the cannibal politicians?"

"No. The bus is parked in the barn, right now. Jinx and Leo are out on a job right now for Pops."

"Who the fuck is Pops?"

Tina took a drink. "He's an old crime boss they work for, when they're not abducting people for the government."

DeVonte said, "Let me hit that whiskey."

She handed him the bottle. He took a drink and gave the bottle back.

She set the bottle on the coffee table. "I'm gonna order some food and have it delivered. You like Chinese?"

DeVonte shrugged. "It's okay."

Muting the TV, Tina reached for an old landline telephone next to the sofa.

Chapter 9

Leo drove. Jinx rode next to him on the passenger's side. Both wore gloves. When they reached their destination, Jinx grabbed the old-fashioned camcorder from the floorboard, and Leo grabbed a scalpel and surgical forceps from the center console.

They got out.

***

Preston Wycliffe loved to read while taking a bath. It was one of his life's most simple, treasured pleasures. It helped him relax, and put him in a mood conducive to sleeping after the routine horrors of a sixteen-hour-shift at the hospital.

Dr. Wycliffe, at fifty-two, looked much younger. He stayed in shape by jogging every day. He was handsome, successful, and popular among the nurses he worked with. He could take his pick of women with whom to be in a relationship, but he was looking for neither a woman nor a relationship. He enjoyed being a bachelor all over again. His kids were grown and gone, and his ex-wife had gotten the house and had since remarried. Preston was alone now, but not the least bit lonely. He could imagine nothing better than coming home to an empty apartment after performing under the bright lights of an operating room.

And so tonight—as every night—he took a hot bath in the Jacuzzi, with a glass of wine and a hardback novel.

And life was good. He lost himself in the world of the novel.

Sometime later, he averted his gaze from the book to take a sip of wine—and saw two men standing in the bathroom. One was black; the other was white. An old-fashioned camcorder dangled from a strap around the black man's neck. The white man held a scalpel in one hand and surgical forceps in the other.

Preston set the novel on the floor next to the tub. "Who are you? How did you get in here? What do you want?"

The white man thrust the scalpel out, clacked the prongs of the forceps together twice, and said nothing.

Dr. Wycliffe, with only the water and the bubbles between him and these two intruders, suddenly felt more vulnerable than he had ever felt. "Who are you?" he repeated. "What do you want?"

"Who we are," the black man said, "and what we want has nothing to do with anything. One of our bosses, however, was paid a large sum of money by a family who wants to see you eat your own testicles."

"What are you talking about?" Preston said.

"Finish your wine," the white man told him. "You'll need it."

Preston drained his glass, and his knees began to shake beneath the bath bubbles.

The black man pointed the camcorder at Preston and clicked it on, then looked at him through its eyepiece. "We have great lighting in this nice, white bathroom. Has anyone ever told you that you're a handsome man? I'm sure the ladies tell you that all the time. It's a shame you'll have to die eating your testicles."

Dr. Wycliffe—clutching an edge of the tub—rose partially from the water, but bath bubbles still concealed his genitals. "I will not just let you kill me."

The white man smiled. "What are you gonna do, doctor? Fight us naked?"

"Yes, if I have to."

"You'll lose, I assure you."

Preston threw his wineglass, but it missed them both and shattered against a mirror.

The white man smiled again. "Nice try."

As the two men approached him, Preston slunk back down into the water as if it could protect him. They each grabbed a fistful of his hair, then yanked him out and began bashing his head against a wall. Soon thereafter, he lost consciousness.

***

Preston came to with a headache, and looked around. Flat on his back, he lay naked with his wrists and ankles handcuffed to the four posts of his own bed. The intruders—now his captors—loomed over him, staring down. The white man held the scalpel and surgical forceps. The black man pointed the camcorder at him; its little red light was flashing.

Preston said, "Can I ask you guys a question?"

"Of course," the white man said.

"Who exactly is paying you to harm me?"

The black man scratched his head, still holding the camcorder. "I already told you: one of our bosses is paying us, but he's being paid by a family who wants to watch you suffer."

"But I have no enemies. Who in the world would want to watch me suffer?"

"Well," the white man said, "by no means am I an educated physician such as yourself, but I'll see if I can solve this conundrum for you. I suspect it's someone related to a person who died in your operating room, and, because they want to watch you eat your own testicles, I'm assuming the procedure you botched had something to *do* with testicles."

"My god," Preston said, in a moment of realization and remembrance—because he *knew*. "The Baxter boy. Little Mattie Baxter. He came in for a routine hernia-removal surgery, and died from a violent reaction to the anesthesia."

The black man lowered the camera. "Yes. I would say that's it exactly. Probably his father." He then covered his head with a leather mask.

"But that wasn't *my* fault. It was *no one's* fault. These things happen. Why are they blaming me for something I had nothing to do with?"

"Hey," the white man said, as he also covered his head with a leather mask, "don't ask us. We're just doing our job." Then he raised the scalpel. "And I'm going to split your scrotum open now."

"Wait," Preston implored, struggling with the handcuffs. "Whatever your boss is paying you, I'll double it."

"Sorry," the black man said.

"I'll triple it! I'll pay you everything I have!"

"Doctor," the white man said, "tonight's the end of the road for you, so you may as well accept it and die with some dignity. But I'd better take my clothes off first. I'd say this is going to get quite messy."

The white man removed his clothes, even stripping out of his socks and boxers, then turned on Preston's bedside stereo system. Classical music began playing at low volume, and the white man turned it up. "To drown out your screams," he explained.

Preston glanced over at the black man, who stood filming him with the camcorder, and then he told the white man, "Please, don't do this."

The white man joined him on the bed. "Are you ready to eat some meatballs, doctor?"

Preston started screaming as the torture, castration, and force-feeding began, and it all went on for quite some time . . .

***

By the time Jinx stopped filming, Leo was covered in blood. The doctor's two hands and two feet were still cuffed to the four posts of the bed, but the rest of his corpse lay scattered throughout the room: stuck to the spattered walls; congealing on the mattress and floor; even hanging like red stalactites from the ceiling.

"I'm gonna go take a shower," Leo said.

Later, while Leo drove them home, Jinx checked his phone on the passenger's side. "Got a message from my brother," he said.

"DeVonte?"

"Yep. He's at the house right now, waiting for us."

"Cool," Leo said, lighting a cigarette. "I'm looking forward to meeting him."

Chapter 10

DeVonte woke from darkened dreams of death and sex to sunlight streaming into his new bedroom. *Fuck,* he thought. *I should've closed the curtains.*

He got up, took a shower in the adjoining bathroom, and brushed his teeth. Then he got dressed and went downstairs.

In the living room, Jinx sat on the sofa, reading a book. He looked up at DeVonte and smiled. "It's good to see you, brother. Sorry I missed you last night. We didn't get home until late."

DeVonte shrugged. "It's all good. That white chick got me drinking some of that cowboy-killer shit, and I guess I passed out."

Jinx laughed. "Yeah, man. Tina definitely likes to drink some whiskey."

A white dude entered the living room wearing a shoulder rig. "You must be DeVonte," he said. "I'm Leo. It's nice to meet you."

DeVonte nodded. "It's nice to meet you, too."

Cracking open a beer, Leo sat down on the loveseat.

Tina came downstairs with the Rottweiler by her side. "I need a ride to Roxanne's house," she announced.

Jinx shot her a look. "Roxanne's back in town?"

"Yep. She just got back last night."

"Whatchu going over there for?"

Tina shrugged. "Just to hang out."

"I thought you two broke up," Jinx said.

Tina shook her head. "No, we just agreed to see other people. You should take me over there. You've been wanting to hook up with Roxanne, anyway."

Closing his book, Jinx rose from the sofa. Then he asked Leo, "You got the keys to the Cadillac?"

Leo tossed him the keys.

Then Jinx told Tina, "Ready when you are."

They left.

Victor dropped to the floor and began gnawing on a rawhide bone.

Leo turned on the TV. "You hungry?" he asked DeVonte. "You want some breakfast?"

"Nah, man, but I could go for one of those beers."

"There's plenty in the fridge. Help yourself."

DeVonte headed toward the kitchen.

Chapter 11

Kaitlyn, eighteen, stood smoking in the greenhouse only because it was raining outside. Beneath the arches of the tempered safety-glass roof, she listened to thunder and watched lightning provide illumination to the dreary morning. She hated being awake this early, but at least the cigarette and the storm lifted her spirits.

She had been working at the greenhouse all summer, ever since high-school graduation, and Kaitlyn had decided long ago that she would not be going to college. While growing up, her mother—a prostitute—had been involved with many men, most of whom were college graduates with more debt than reward for their financed education.

Kaitlyn finished her cigarette and stomped it out in the pea gravel beneath a tray of red roses, pink carnations, and lavender orchids.

This job's not too bad, she thought.

With high school behind her, however, she knew she needed to figure out what to do with the rest of her life.

As Kaitlyn stood misting a row of marigolds, John Gardner—owner of the greenhouse—rushed inside from the storm. His wife, Jenny, followed him in beneath a yellow umbrella, which she quickly closed.

"Good morning, Kaitlyn," John said. "That's some terrible weather out there. I'm glad you could make it in today."

Kaitlyn smiled. "The storm will pass."

Jenny propped her umbrella against a safety-glass wall. "Yes, and not soon enough when it does."

Kaitlyn turned around, bent over, and set the spray-mister down, knowing that John and Jenny *both* were admiring her ass. Each was sleeping with Kaitlyn behind the other's back, and neither had any knowledge of their spouse's infidelity.

Time passed, and the rain abated at noon. Soon thereafter, John offered to drive downtown and purchase lunch for all three of them.

"Thanks, honey," his wife said. "I'm starving."

He nodded. "Very well. I'll be back in thirty minutes."

John left, and then Jenny asked Kaitlyn, "Wanna get naked?"

"I would love to."

Kaitlyn followed Jenny into the office behind the greenhouse.

Chapter 12

Jinx drove. Tina rode next to him on the passenger's side.

As they headed to Roxanne's mansion in the Santa Monica Mountains, Jinx glanced over at the old Hawthorn Hotel to his left. "Didn't you tell me that place was haunted?"

Tina turned the stereo down. "It's haunted as fuck."

"That's where you met Roxanne, right?"

"Yep. She likes to go have drinks there in the lounge, just to get out of her house. And she also rents a suite there sometimes, to work on whatever book she's working on. You know, just for a change of scenery. The Hawthorn's like her home away from home."

It was noon by the time they arrived at Roxanne's estate, and the gate at the bottom of her driveway was open. Jinx drove the Cadillac up the mountain. At the top, he parked behind a Mercedes in front of the mansion, and they got out.

Roxanne greeted them at the main entrance. "Hello, Tina. Who's your friend?"

"This is Jinx," Tina said. "One of my two roommates I was telling you about. Well, *three* roommates, now."

"It's nice to meet you, Jinx. I'm Roxanne. Come on in." She stepped aside.

Tina entered the foyer, and Jinx followed her in. Then Roxanne closed the door and led them into the great room.

Jinx looked around: white-and-gold marble floor; antique furniture; a grand piano in a corner of the room; two spiral staircases with an elevator between them; a coffered ceiling thirty feet above; limestone columns along the back wall, beyond which lay an infinity pool visible through the floor-to-ceiling windows.

"Nice place," he told Roxanne.

"Thanks." She approached a minibar next to the sofa. "Would you two like a drink?"

"Not me," Tina said. "I gotta go."

Jinx shot her a look. "What are you talking about?"

"I'm meeting someone at the Hawthorn."

"The Hawthorn?"

"Yep."

"Then why did we come here? We just passed the Hawthorn. You told me you wanted to come here and hang out."

Tina shrugged. "That was a lie. It was all part of my master plan to get you two together. Enjoy your day." She headed toward the foyer.

Jinx glanced at Roxanne, who stood looking perplexed with a hand on her hip. Then he asked Tina, "Do you need me to drop you off at the Hawthorn?"

"No thanks. I'll walk."

Seconds later, he heard the front door open and close as Tina left.

"Well," he said, "this got awkward fast."

Roxanne shook her head. "Not really. It's unexpected, but it doesn't have to be awkward at all."

Her minibar featured an under-the-counter refrigerator, and she opened it. "I'm gonna start with a beer, since it's only noon. Would you like a beer?"

"I guess."

She grabbed two beers, gave one to Jinx, and then pointed toward the sofa. "Have a seat."

Jinx sat down and cracked open his beer.

Roxanne sat down next to him and opened her beer, too. Then she raised her bottle. "To a new friendship."

He shrugged. "I suppose we'll see."

They drank, and he was pleased to see a cigarette lighter and an ashtray on her coffee table.

"So, tell me something about yourself," Roxanne said.

"What do you wanna know?"

"All kinds of things. Do you date white women?"

Jinx lit a cigarette. "I don't actually *do* a lot of dating, but I've definitely fucked a lot of white women."

"Oh really?"

"Yes. I just don't usually trust people enough to be in relationships."

"Ah, so you have trust issues."

"Well, I don't know about all that, but let's just say that I've been burned a time or two in the past."

"By women?"

"Yes, by women."

They sipped their beers in silence momentarily, then Roxanne said, "Tina mentioned a new roommate. Who's the new roommate?"

"My brother."

"Brother?"

"Yes. DeVonte. He just came down to L.A. from San Francisco."

"Do you trust your brother?"

Jinx took a drink. "Of course I trust my brother."

"But you don't trust women."

"No, I don't. That's different."

"It's *not* different," Roxanne said. "And I don't trust anybody, by the way. Not even myself."

He nodded. "I like your style."

"I'm switching to whiskey." Roxanne rose from the sofa. "Would you like one?"

"Nah, I'd better not. I still have to drive."

"No, you don't. You can stay here with me." Then she smiled at him, and added, "Besides, I won't bite unless you want me to."

Jinx stubbed his cigarette out. "In that case, make it a double."

Chapter 13

While Jenny shopped for groceries (a task that guaranteed her absence for at least an hour), Kaitlyn lay beneath John while he fucked her on his bed with as much passion as his wife did when he wasn't home. Both John and Jenny remained clueless to each other's infidelity, and Kaitlyn was getting tired of the whole affair.

Finally, John finished. After he caught his breath, he looked into her eyes and said, "I love you."

I don't believe in love, Kaitlyn thought, but didn't say it.

"I have some money put aside," John told her. "I want to divorce Jenny and move away. Will you come with me?"

"Maybe," Kaitlyn said. "But you need to put some clothes on. Your wife will be home soon."

Rising from the bed, John began getting dressed.

***

Later that evening, while John played poker elsewhere with his friends, Kaitlyn and Jenny made love atop a blanket on the greenhouse floor. The sun had already set, and the fading light of dusk cast faint illumination through the clear roof and safety-glass walls.

At some point, the overhead lights came on unexpectedly.

Then Kaitlyn—with Jenny's face buried between her thighs—heard John yell, "Kaitlyn! Oh my god, Kaitlyn! How could you?"

Jenny raised her head and turned to face her husband. "Why did you say Kaitlyn's name instead of mine?"

Ignoring his wife, John told Kaitlyn, "I thought you loved me! We were planning a future together! How could you do this to me?"

Jenny and Kaitlyn rose from the floor, both naked.

Then Jenny asked Kaitlyn, "Have you been fucking my husband?"

Kaitlyn did not reply.

"She's been playing us for fools, Jenny," John said. "Let's kill this fucking bitch."

Kaitlyn attempted to get dressed, but John and Jenny attacked her. Jenny began slapping Kaitlyn's breasts, then John smacked her across an eye, knocking her down. Kaitlyn rolled beneath a bench of roses to get away from them. The pea gravel abraded her bare skin. When she sprang to her feet on the other side, she saw John and Jenny rushing around opposite ends of the bench toward her, closing in fast.

Looking for something to use as a weapon, Kaitlyn saw an empty bucket, a shovel, a rake, and a steel tomato stake. She grabbed the tomato stake and hoisted it with both hands like a baseball bat. "Leave me alone!"

Jenny came running at her with a garden spade, screaming in a fit of rage. Kaitlyn swung the tomato stake at Jenny's head and connected, silencing her screams with the sound of cracking bone. Jenny dropped to the floor, twitching in a spreading pool of blood, then lay still.

John glared at Kaitlyn, furious. "You fucking bitch."

"Stay away from me," Kaitlyn said.

John knelt down next to his wife, checking for a pulse. "She's dead." He then retrieved the garden spade lying next to Jenny's corpse.

"I'm warning you," Kaitlyn told him. "Leave me alone."

John stood up and hurled the garden spade at Kaitlyn. It hurt when it bounced off her shoulder, but she didn't drop the tomato stake.

Then he lunged at her with outstretched hands.

Instead of swinging the stake, Kaitlyn gripped it like a sword and thrust it as hard as she could into his genital region, which took the fight right out of him. John put his hands down over his crotch and doubled over, howling.

"Shut up!" Kaitlyn said. "Before someone calls the police."

John did not comply, and she smacked him alongside the head with the tomato stake. He crashed onto the floor, bleeding, and screamed more loudly than before.

Then Kaitlyn felt something inside herself snap. She wanted silence immediately, and began swinging the tomato stake. When she finally stopped, John's head and face were nothing more than gory smears of unrecognizable features.

Kaitlyn paused for a moment to contemplate what had just occurred. *Double homicide,* she thought. *And it may have been self-defense, but who would believe me? Especially with John's head smashed to smithereens?*

Kaitlyn wasn't a juvenile anymore. She was eighteen going on eighty, as her mother (*the devil's whore*) so often said, and Kaitlyn refused to stick around and be charged with double homicide.

Fortunately, there were no security cameras around.

She got dressed and washed her fingerprints off the tomato stake while wearing a pair of pruning gloves. Then she grabbed the garden spade and rammed it through John's head before placing it in his dead wife's hand. *There,* she thought. *Hopefully, that will be enough to confuse the investigators.*

In a shed behind the building, she found some gasoline and splashed it throughout the greenhouse. Before she left, Kaitlyn shut off the automatic watering systems. Then she struck a match and set a row of bellflowers on fire.

Once in her car and speeding out of the parking lot, Kaitlyn risked a glance into the rearview: the greenhouse was in flames.

Soon it would be consumed.

Chapter 14

"What's your name?" the man asked Tina, in the lounge at the Hawthorn Hotel. He had a huge, nasty-looking (apparently the wound was still bleeding) bandage on his hand, but he otherwise seemed okay.

"Tina," she said. "What happened to your hand?"

"I'm Kirk. And I slammed it in a car door."

"Sounds painful."

"It was."

"Looks painful, too."

He shrugged. "Yeah, well, the doctor prescribed me some good medication, so I'm not feeling any pain." He sipped his drink. "I'm not supposed to be drinking on the medicine, of course. But you only live once, right?"

She smiled. "Now that, Kirk, I'm not so sure about."

He laughed. Tina thought he sounded a little nervous.

"Can I buy you a drink?" he said.

"Sure."

"What are you drinking?"

She sipped her cocktail. "This is a cosmopolitan."

"Be right back." He walked to the bar.

She watched him order two drinks and bring them to her table.

"Mind if I join you?" he said.

"Be my guest."

Kirk sat down.

"Do you come here often?" Tina asked him.

Kirk cocked his head. "We're in a hotel. Why would I come here often?"

Tina shrugged. "I don't know. I had a girlfriend who used to live here. And I had another girlfriend who likes to stay here from time to time"—she pointed to the west—"even though she has a house up there in the hills."

Kirk sipped his drink. "That's kinda weird."

"Not really. She's a famous writer."

"Ah, okay. There's probably a lot of those in this town. I'm not from around here. I'm just passing through. And you don't sound like you're from around here, either."

"I'm not," Tina said. "And right now, I'm looking to score some heroin."

"Heroin?"

"Yes. You wouldn't happen to have any, would you?"

"No, but I have a bunch of other drugs up in my room."

"What kinda drugs?"

Kirk sipped his drink. "Coke, meth, pills, DMT—"

"Oh my god," Tina said. "I've been wanting to try DMT forever."

"You've never done it?"

"No. Will you do some with me?"

Kirk smiled. "Sure, I can do that."

They finished their drinks and took an elevator up to his suite on the fourteenth floor.

Tina looked around: clothes tumbling out of a suitcase next to the bed; empty liquor bottles and room-service trays all over the place; beer cans turned into ashtrays; a mirror frosted with white powder on the coffee table; a baggie of what looked like crack rocks and a glass pipe on the floor.

Kirk picked up the baggie and the glass pipe and set them on the coffee table. "Have a seat."

Tina sat down on the couch. "So, you're just passing through?"

Kirk crossed the room. "Yep." From his suitcase, he withdrew another sandwich baggie, and then joined her on the couch. "I'm from Oregon, originally. What about you?"

"Virginia," Tina said.

"Damn, you're a long way from home."

Tina shook her head. "No, I'm not. This is my home, now."

Kirk pinched some white crystals from the sandwich baggie and placed them in the glass pipe. "It's a cool place to visit, but L.A.'s just too damn big for me."

After he lit the pipe, they passed it back and forth a couple of times.

And then, boom, Tina got blasted. The DMT hit her brain and she felt amazing, as if someone had shot her in the head with not a bullet but positive energy. She also felt that she had entered another dimension, one in which the fabric of reality was a kaleidoscope of bright colors and rapidly moving images.

But then—just like that—Tina found herself surrounded by strangers, as if she had blinked and the hotel suite became filled with people she didn't know. *Where did they all come from?* she wondered. *And how did they all arrive here so suddenly?*

Then people began removing their clothes, and they started yelling to Kirk that he should take his clothes off, too.

Kirk shot her a look. "Come on, Tina! Let's get naked!"

As Kirk removed his clothes, Tina felt an icy rage gushing through her brain. "Stay away from me," she told him. "Goddamn freak."

But Kirk did not stay away. Instead, he pounced with the speed of a cheetah and slammed her to the floor.

While several naked people held Tina down, another person handed Kirk a hypodermic syringe. Smiling, he jammed its needle into her neck and pressed the plunger.

After that, things got blurry . . .

***

Tina didn't know if she had lost consciousness or not, but when her vision cleared, she found herself naked, gagged, and strapped to a metal chair in a large room that looked like a laboratory with mirrors on the walls.

What the fuck?

Apparently, they had moved her from the hotel suite to a different location.

Casting her gaze around the naked people surrounding her, Tina's jaws ached from the ball-gag crammed inside her mouth, and the bright lights of the room made her eyes hurt.

Then Kirk—now as completely naked as everyone else—parked a wheeled, stainless-steel table next to her chair. Atop the table lay knives, power tools, and surgical instruments. Tina would have lunged for one of those knives if her wrists had not been strapped by leather cuffs to the arms of the chair.

"We're gonna have a whole lot of fun," Kirk told her. "And by *we,* I mean everyone in this room except for you. This will not be fun for you at all."

He shoved her chair in front of a full-length mirror. "I want you to see everything we do," he explained. "So keep your eyes open. If you close your eyes, I'll cut your eyelids off. Do you understand me?"

Tina nodded.

He then grabbed a fistful of her hair and yanked it out by its roots. The pain was intense, and Tina would have called him a piece of shit had her mouth not been gagged.

"We need you bald," Kirk told her, "for what we're gonna do."

The other naked people needed no further instructions. One by one, they grabbed fistfuls of her hair and pulled it out, laughing while Tina wept as she watched them toss bloody clumps of her hair onto the floor.

Soon, she was totally bald.

Moving the metal table closer to her chair, Kirk withdrew a scalpel from its surface and held it up. The scalpel's blade glinted beneath the bright, overhead lights. To Tina, it looked like the blade of a guillotine.

He then circled around her and put a hand on her shoulder, giving Tina a clear view of herself in the mirror while Kirk stood behind her.

Using the scalpel, he sliced a red line all the way around her head, precisely where a headband would be placed. Setting the scalpel down, he used both hands to peel her scalp off, and then tossed it onto the floor. From the metal table, he picked up what Tina believed was a craniotomy drill, the sound of which filled the room when he turned it on. Soon thereafter, white chips of bone misted the air as he drilled into her skull.

Perhaps a minute later, he set the drill down and picked up a power saw, which had a small, circular blade. When he squeezed its trigger, the saw's loud, piercing screech made Tina try to grind her teeth despite the ball-gag in her mouth.

He worked the saw's blade around her skull the same way he had with the scalpel: cutting a line where a headband would be placed. After encircling her entire skull, he set the saw back down on the metal table.

Using both hands, he removed her skullcap, which came off like a hat, and Tina shuddered. The half-dome of her exposed brain glistened a bright, pinkish white. Clear fluid dribbled off her brain and down her bloodsoaked face.

Smiling at Tina in the mirror, Kirk raised her skullcap and told the naked spectators, "I'll turn this into a soup bowl later."

He set her skullcap on the table and picked up a knife. "We're going to eat your brains now," he told her.

Using his free hand, he slipped some fingers beneath her brain and slightly raised it. Then he used the knife to slice off a piece of her brain and held it up. Turning to one of the women standing next to him, Kirk said, "You get the first bite."

Smiling, the woman shoved the morsel into her mouth, moaning in ecstasy while she chewed. "Delicious," she said, once she had swallowed.

After that, Kirk removed segments of Tina's brain and fed them to the spectators one by one.

How much longer, Tina wondered, *until I'm a ghost? Hopefully I'll get my skullcap back.*

Her peripheral vision vanished, and her remaining tunnel vision faded to pinpoints of light.

Then everything went black.

***

She came to standing up in the hotel suite, fully dressed. Kirk lay slaughtered on the floor. He had been stabbed at least a hundred times, and his blood was splattered all over the walls, the couch, the coffee table, the floor—even the ceiling.

Tina looked down at the folding knife in her hand, which was covered in blood, as were her clothes. *Damn,* she thought. *Was all of that just a vivid hallucination? If so, DMT is one hell of a drug.*

Stripping out of her bloody clothes, she took a shower in the adjoining bathroom. Then she washed Kirk's blood off her knife in the kitchenette, put her own clothes in a trash bag, and dressed in one of Kirk's T-shirts and a pair of his sweatpants.

Before she left, Tina searched the suite, finding a bottle of OxyContin in the bathroom, a sandwich baggie of cocaine hidden in the couch, and a stack of hundred-dollar bills in Kirk's suitcase. She counted the cash: five thousand dollars exactly. She put the money, the coke, and the pills in her pocket.

Back downstairs, the lobby was empty. She thought about returning to the lounge for another drink, but decided against it.

She went outside. The sun was shining.

She took off walking.

Chapter 15

After killing John and Jenny, Kaitlyn brought her car to a screeching halt in front of her mother's house. Stepping out onto the driveway, she heard sirens in the distance and knew there would be no saving the greenhouse. She hoped the fire would burn each body to a crisp and eradicate all evidence of the murders.

Covered in blood, she rushed inside the house to take a shower.

The house was small, and she heard her mother screaming in pleasure as soon as she stepped inside. *She must be on the clock,* Kaitlyn thought. *She only makes that much noise when she's fucking someone for money.*

Her mother's bedroom door was closed, but Kaitlyn heard the twang of bedsprings and the headboard smacking the wall. She was thankful her mother was too busy working to see her coming home covered in blood.

Kaitlyn showered quickly, washing blood out of her hair and scrubbing her fingernails, then put her bloodstained outfit in a plastic bag and dressed in clean clothes. She packed a few favorite outfits into her suitcase, then tied the plastic bag and shoved it inside the suitcase, too. *I can't leave those bloody clothes here,* she thought. *The police will be here asking about John and Jenny soon, but I'll be long gone by then.*

Kaitlyn looked around her room, knowing she would likely never see this place again.

She had been saving money for a newer car, but that would have to wait. She pulled a shoebox from beneath her bed and counted the cash within: three thousand dollars—plenty enough money to leave town with.

She gathered her journals, her notebooks of poetry, and a few books for the road. Before she left the room, Kaitlyn made sure that she had her fake ID, which listed her as twenty-one, old enough to buy alcohol—and yes: the fake ID was in her purse. She crammed her purse into the suitcase and closed it.

In the living room, she turned for one last glance at the home to which she would likely never return—and heard a man say, "Who's your daddy, bitch?" as he smacked her mother's ass.

Kaitlyn left, heading south with the windows down and the radio off, enjoying the night wind in her wet hair.

I killed two people tonight, she thought. *Am I a murderer? Or was it self-defense? And why did it feel so good?*

She was overcome with wonder and dread simultaneously. Her life was an open book, filled with limitless possibilities, but she would have to become a new person to avoid apprehension.

Maybe I'll get a job in a strip club under a fake name.

Kaitlyn just hoped her rusty car would make it to California.

Chapter 16

On the sofa, Leo finished his whiskey and set the bottle on the coffee table. He needed to go get more, but Jinx had left a few hours ago to drive Tina to Roxanne's house, and he had still not returned with the Cadillac.

"I'd love to know where the fuck your brother is," he told DeVonte, who sat on the loveseat to his left in the living room. They had been watching TV and had barely spoken to each other at all.

DeVonte shrugged. "Give him a call."

"I sent him a text," Leo said, "but he hasn't replied. I need to go to the liquor store, and I don't feel like driving the goddamn bus."

DeVonte shot him a look. "I heard y'all have a lot of fun on that bus."

"I take it you talked to Tina," Leo said.

"Yeah, man. She told me some crazy shit about you and my brother."

"What all did she tell you?"

"That you and Jinx picked her up in Virginia, with a bunch of people handcuffed to poles inside the bus, then dropped them off as food for politicians in Washington, D.C."

Leo nodded. "That's about the gist of it. And here's the thing: those cannibal politicians might call us at any time and tell us to bring them some more food, and then Jinx and I will have to hit the road. That's why it's pissing me off that he won't answer his phone."

DeVonte lit a cigarette. "I'm sure he has his reasons."

"I guess it doesn't matter," Leo said. "If they call, I can just take you with me. I mean, if I tell the people I'm working for that you're Jinx's brother, they won't give a fuck. Unless, of course, you'd have a problem with abducting people from the highways while traveling east."

DeVonte shook his head. "Nah, man, I ain't got no problem with that. And I can give you a ride to the liquor store, by the way."

"Cool, man. Thanks." Rising from the sofa, Leo glanced over at Victor, who lay on the floor next to the door, gnawing on a rawhide bone. "I'll need to grab some food for the dog while we're out. He likes cheeseburgers."

DeVonte rose from the loveseat. "I like cheeseburgers, too."

"Cool," Leo said.

They left.

Chapter 17

After sex, Jinx lay next to Roxanne in her bedroom on the mansion's second floor. They passed a bottle of whiskey back and forth, smoking cigarettes, then Jinx told her, "I finished your novel *Gossamer* recently. I really enjoyed it."

"*Gossamer*'s not even out yet," Roxanne said.

"I know, but Tina had a copy and emailed it to me, and I read it on my phone."

"Ah, okay. Do you like to read a lot?"

"Yes, I do."

"What do you like to read?"

"Just whatever." Jinx took a drink. "Right now I'm reading a biography about the Plaster Casters."

"Plaster Casters? Are they a rock band?"

"No, they were two women from Chicago, a long time ago, who made plaster casts of rock stars' penises."

"That's weird," Roxanne said.

"I know. It's a Plasters Casters biography, but there's a lot of interviews with other groupies scattered throughout the book. And, according to some of those groupies, Huey Lewis had one of the biggest penises of all the famous rock stars."

"Is that so?"

"Yep. They'd ask a groupie about such-and-such rock star, and the groupie would be like, 'Oh, he's big, but he's no Huey.' Then they'd ask another groupie about someone else, and they'd say the same thing: 'He's big, but he's no Huey.' Apparently the dude was hung like an elephant's trunk."

Roxanne stubbed her cigarette out. "Was he a black guy?"

"Nope. As white as you. He was a pop star back in the 1980s. You've seriously never heard of Huey Lewis?"

Roxanne shook her head. "I don't think so." She then rolled over to face him and squeezed his penis. "But, for what it's worth, you're *definitely* a Huey."

Jinx took a drink and set the bottle on the nightstand. "You ready for round two?"

Roxanne smiled. "I'm always ready."

Chapter 18

Kaitlyn's car made it across the California border, but just barely. The engine had been missing and making strange noises for miles, and it finally died with a bang in Crescent City. She coasted to a stop not far from an off-ramp, turned on the hazard lights, and got out.

The night was warm. Minimal traffic moved beneath a starless sky. The air smelled of diesel fumes and monoxides. Kaitlyn lit a cigarette and stuck her thumb out.

A black van passed by, slowed down, and then pulled over in the distance.

She fetched her suitcase from the car, jogged to the van's passenger side, and opened the door. "My car died. How far are you going?"

"Not far," the man behind the steering wheel said. "But I can at least get you off the side of the road. Hop on in."

Kaitlyn could see his face beneath the overhead dome light. He was attractive, but much older than she was. He appeared to be about forty, with dark hair and dark eyes. He wore blue jeans and a black jacket.

Kaitlyn put her suitcase behind the passenger's seat and got in. "Thanks." She closed the door.

"No problem. Where you headed?"

"Los Angeles." A pause. "To visit friends," she added—which was a lie: Kaitlyn didn't know anyone in California.

"Wanna go to a service station? See if you can get your car towed?"

"No. It's not even worth it." She thought about the double homicide she committed earlier. "What I really need is a good strong drink."

The man shot her a look. "Are you even old enough to drink?"

No, Kaitlyn thought, *but I'm eighteen, so I'm old enough to fuck.* "I'm twenty-one," she lied, but it was a lie that her fake ID could back up.

The man turned to face her, and smiled. His eyes glanced down to soak in the swell of her breasts. "Wanna go to a bar? Have a few drinks? Try to figure out what you're gonna do?"

"Sure. I'd love to go to a bar with you. I'm Kaitlyn, by the way."

"It's nice to meet you. I'm Alex Gray."

He took her to a small club called The Velvet Web and parked his van around back amongst economy cars, pickup trucks, motorcycles, and SUVs.

Kaitlyn said, "My money's in the suitcase."

Alex shook his head. "Keep it. Drinks are on me."

"Thanks!"

Kaitlyn grabbed her fake ID from the purse inside her suitcase, but a bouncer let them enter the club without even checking it.

The interior was packed, and the music was loud. Kaitlyn followed Alex to the bar, where two bartenders worked furiously to meet the demands of the drinkers. *For such a small place,* Kaitlyn thought, *The Velvet Web sure is happening.*

She and Alex jostled for attention at the end of the bar. After their drinks were served, they drank without speaking. Kaitlyn thought about how she could never go home again after killing John and Jenny.

Later, after numerous rounds of whiskey and beer, Kaitlyn said, "Let's get out of here."

They left. Alex stopped at a store for a twelve-pack. Kaitlyn stayed in the van.

Back on the road. Rock music on the radio. They didn't talk much. Alex drank beer while he drove. Kaitlyn drank beer and chain-smoked cigarettes on the passenger's side.

Sometime later, Alex parked his van by a river beneath a bridge in another town.

Kaitlyn said, "I hope you have some condoms."

Alex killed the engine. Then he slipped his hands into some gloves and punched her in the face.

***

Kaitlyn woke up naked with a headache in the back of the van. She tasted blood in her mouth. Alex loomed over her, smiling beneath a lamp that illuminated the cargo space. She lay on a mattress, with her hands tied behind her back. She tried to free her hands, but didn't succeed. *It's not a rope,* she thought. *He tied my wrists with my own silk panties.*

Her legs were free, but Alex sat astride her upper thighs, pinning her down. She saw madness in his eyes, an insanity to which she felt attracted. Excluding his gloves, Alex—like Kaitlyn—was totally naked. His erect penis jutted only inches away from her face. He held a bottle of beer in one hand and a butcher's knife in the other.

Kaitlyn spat blood out of her mouth. Then she returned his smile. "Penny for your thoughts."

He laughed.

"Nice teeth," she told him. "And the head of your penis looks like a goddamn lemon."

Alex finished his beer and set the bottle next to the mattress.

Then he raised the knife. "And you'll look better after I cut your tits off. After you're opened up, all wet and red."

Kaitlyn wrestled with the panties that bound her wrists behind her back. "You shouldn't make promises you can't keep."

Alex cocked his head. "Something tells me that you actually *enjoy* a little pain."

"I do." Suddenly, her wrists slipped free of the panties. She kept her hands behind her back. "But I don't wanna die. Not tonight. If you put the knife away, I'll give you the best blowjob you've ever had in your life."

Smiling, Alex rubbed his chin with the handle of the knife. "I'll tell you what: if you give me the best blowjob I've ever had, I'll let you live. If it's not the best blowjob I've ever had, I will kill you. Do we have a deal?"

"Yes, but put the knife away first. It's making me nervous. I don't want it to affect my performance."

He tossed the knife aside. Then he leaned forward, and she took a few inches of his penis into her mouth. "Suck it good, bitch," he told her. "If you don't, I'll kill you nice and slow."

With her head raised, Kaitlyn sucked until her neck started cramping, then stopped and lowered her head onto the mattress. "Just lay on my face and fuck me in the mouth."

Alex did, cramming the entire length of his erection down her throat. He began pumping.

As he grunted and moaned, Kaitlyn yanked both hands from beneath her back and clutched his ass cheeks.

He stopped and withdrew his penis from her mouth. "I suppose I didn't tie those panties tight enough."

Kaitlyn smiled. "What's the matter? Are you afraid of me?"

"Nope." He shoved his penis back into her mouth.

Kaitlyn knew this man intended to kill her. She counted to three, took a deep breath through her nostrils, and then bit down so hard that her upper and lower teeth connected. She tasted blood immediately, even before Alex began to scream.

As he thrashed and flailed about, Kaitlyn bit down again, harder, clenching and grinding her teeth. Then she jerked her head to the left, and his penis ripped from his body. She spat it out and was sluiced in a fountain of blood.

Clutching his bleeding wound, Alex rolled off the mattress, screaming.

Kaitlyn sprang from the mattress and saw the knife on the floor of the van. As she grabbed it, Alex charged her. She rammed the knife into his stomach, and he yelled. She yanked it out and he fell onto the mattress.

As Alex lay bleeding, Kaitlyn straddled him.

"Please," he whispered. "The keys are in the ignition. Just take me to a hospital."

Kaitlyn raised the knife, smiling. "I told you I give good head."

Then she slaughtered him, stabbing him so many times she lost count, still plunging the blade deep into his eyes, neck, and chest long after he was dead.

Exhausted, she plopped down on the bloodsoaked mattress.

I've killed three people tonight, she thought. *But all three murders had been in self-defense, right? John and Jenny tried to kill me in the greenhouse, and Alex was going to kill me here in this van. But why did I enjoy killing them so much?*

Her mother's voice popped into her head: *"Because you're a psychopath, that's why."*

Kaitlyn laughed.

Still naked, she dragged Alex's body out of the van beneath the bridge, then walked down to the river. At the water's edge, she washed his blood off her body in the moonlight.

Back in the van, she got dressed and sat down behind the steering wheel. The keys were in the ignition, and there was almost a full tank of gas.

I don't even know what town this is, Kaitlyn thought.

She started the engine and headed south toward Los Angeles.

Chapter 19

In her bedroom on the second floor of the compound's main house, Tina finished the book she was reading and set it on her nightstand. Then she took the last drink of Jack Daniel's in her bottle and dropped the empty fifth into her trash can.

"Need to go get more whiskey," she told Victor, who lay on the floor next to her bed. The Rottweiler—gnawing on a rawhide bone—didn't acknowledge her.

Rising from the bed, she headed toward the hallway. Victor got up and followed her down the stairs.

In the living room, DeVonte sat on the sofa, watching TV.

Leo sat on the loveseat, cleaning a disassembled pistol. The grip of another pistol was visible in the shoulder rig he wore.

Tina joined DeVonte on the sofa. "Where's your brother?"

He shrugged. "No idea."

"Probably at Roxanne's," Leo said, without looking up. "Apparently, she and Jinx are an item now."

Tina smiled. "How romantic."

Leo shot her a look. "He needs to bring the Cadillac here and leave it, because I don't have anything to drive except for the bus. And I'm not driving that bus until I have to."

DeVonte asked Tina, "Do you need a ride somewhere?"

She nodded. "Yep. Just to the liquor store."

"I'll take you," DeVonte said.

Leo rose from the loveseat. "I wanna go, too. I'll finish cleaning this gun when we get back." He grabbed his jacket from the floor and put it on.

At the front door, before they left, Tina told Victor, "I'll bring you some cheeseburgers for dinner."

On the floor in front of the TV, Victor looked up from his bone and wagged his tail.

DeVonte drove. Leo rode next to him on the passenger's side. Tina rode behind them in the back.

At the liquor store, DeVonte waited in the car while Tina and Leo went inside. Tina purchased two bottles of whiskey and a carton of cigarettes. Leo bought a half-gallon of rum and a case of beer.

On their way back to the compound, they stopped at a fast-food joint to get cheeseburgers for Victor. While waiting in line at the drive-through, Leo—sitting in front of Tina on the passenger's side—pointed to his right. "Check out the tits on that chick."

Casting her gaze in that direction, Tina saw a teenage girl sitting atop a suitcase next to a payphone. "I think I'm in love."

"You should go talk to her," Leo said. "See if she wants to hang out. I'll pay for Victor's cheeseburgers."

Tina got out of the car. The night was warm. A sickle moon sliced through the darkness above the parking lot.

She approached the teenage girl, who sat smoking a cigarette atop her suitcase.

Tina put one of her own cigarettes in her mouth. "Got a light?" she asked the girl, even though she had a lighter in her pocket.

"Sure." The girl handed her a lighter.

Tina lit the cigarette and gave the lighter back. "I'm Tina. What's your name?"

"Kaitlyn. I just got into town about an hour ago."

Tina looked at the girl's suitcase, and then back into her eyes. "Are you waiting for someone to pick you up?"

"Yes. I called a cab, but I'm still waiting."

"Where are you headed?"

Kaitlyn shrugged. "Nearest hotel, I guess."

"How did you get here?"

"Long story."

Tina smiled. "You should come stay with me. We can get fucked up, and do some fucked-up things."

Kaitlyn cocked her head. "How do you know I'm not a serial killer?"

"I don't, but you look awfully young. How old are you? Sixteen? Seventeen?"

"I'm eighteen," Kaitlyn said. "How old are you?"

"Twenty. And for all you know, I could be a serial killer, too."

"That's true." Finished with her cigarette, Kaitlyn flicked it aside. "So what do you have, anyway? To get fucked up with?"

"Lots of drugs and lots of booze. I live at a compound with some friends not too far from here."

Rising from her suitcase, Kaitlyn picked it up. "Cool," she said. "Let's do it."

Chapter 20

Jinx lay reading next to Roxanne in her bedroom while she wrote.

She closed her laptop, got up, and walked over to the minibar. "I'm in the mood for a vodka tonic. Would you like one?"

"Sure." He closed his book and set it on the nightstand.

Moments later, she returned with two drinks and gave him one.

He sipped it; thought: *Perfect.*

"I've been meaning to ask you something," Jinx said.

She stretched out next to him on the bed. "Oh yeah? What's that?"

He took another drink. "Before I met you, when you and Tina agreed to see other people, she told me that you said you were too dangerous for her, that there was a lot about you that she didn't know. What did you mean by that?"

Roxanne sipped her drink. "That's a tricky question to answer, so I'll start by asking you a question. Do you believe in evolution, or do you think we were created?"

"Created," Jinx said. "Although I don't necessarily believe in God. I think those people who believe that the universe was created in six days about six thousand years ago are out of their goddamn minds."

Roxanne nodded. "I agree. I suppose my beliefs run parallel with the Intelligent Design theory, which holds that a higher power guided the entire creation process, although it's none of our business to consider what that higher power might be. But I *do* know this: there's a whole lot of goodness and light in the universe, but there's also a lot of darkness and evil. And there's a lot of darkness and evil in me."

"Same here," Jinx said. "And there's a lot of darkness and evil in Tina, too."

Placing an ashtray between them on the bed, Roxanne lit a cigarette. "Do you know who Ray Bradbury was?"

"Of course. He was the author of *The Martian Chronicles, Something Wicked This Way Comes,* and a bunch of other stuff."

"That's right. My favorite's *Dandelion Wine,* by the way. Anyway, I sometimes watch old interviews with dead authors on YouTube, and I once heard Ray Bradbury say something that has stuck with me ever since: that there was no use having a universe filled with gazillions of stars if there was no one here to see it. He said that we were the audience; that we were here to witness and celebrate the miraculous. And I agree with Ray Bradbury. But I also agree with one of the beliefs I discovered in Norse mythology."

Jinx sipped his drink. "What's the belief?"

"That the gods," Roxanne said, "don't want us to worship them. Instead, they want us to fight hard and to live long lives, so that we'll have great stories to tell them in the afterlife. But here's the thing: for me, the more fucked up and twisted a story is, the more

I enjoy it. So I've made it my life's mission to make my stories as fucked up and as twisted as possible—both in my fiction *and* in my reality. Do you understand what I'm saying?"

Jinx shot her a look. "I'm thinking that maybe I do. Are you saying that you kill people in both your stories *and* in your real life?"

"It's a two-way street," Roxanne said. "Yes, we're the audience of the universe. We're here to witness the universe, but the universe is also watching us. Are you familiar with Chuck Palahniuk?"

Jinx nodded. "Of course. He's the author of *Fight Club*."

"Yes, although my favorite by him is *Invisible Monsters*. And there's a passage from that book in which Palahniuk wrote something like: *'God watches us and kills us when we get boring, so we must never, ever become boring.'* And the universe itself is a murderer. The universe has only one supreme goal, and that is the death, destruction, and total annihilation of everything. So when I write my stories, and when I kill people in real life, I'm simply trying to stay alive. I'm trying to keep the universe entertained. I'm trying not to become boring so the universe won't kill me. Does that make sense?"

Jinx finished his drink. "Makes perfect sense to me. And if Palahniuk's theory is true, I should live to be a very old man."

Roxanne cocked her head. "Do you kill people, too?"

He laughed. "What do you think?"

She smiled. "I think I told you my story, so now it's time for you to tell me yours."

He raised his empty glass. "Will you make me another drink first?"

Rising from the bed, Roxanne took his glass and headed toward the minibar.

Chapter 21

In the car, Kaitlyn rode behind the black dude—DeVonte—who drove. The white dude, Leo, rode next to him on the passenger's side. Tina, who sat to Kaitlyn's right, had introduced her to the two men as soon as they climbed inside.

Leo fired up a joint, and they passed it around.

Soon thereafter, they arrived at a compound atop a hill overlooking a cemetery. DeVonte parked his car in front of the main house, and they got out.

"This is where you live?" Kaitlyn asked, sweeping her gaze across the property at the cabins, barns, and other buildings.

"Yep," Leo said. "Home sweet home."

"Nice," Kaitlyn said.

She followed the three of them into the main house—where the largest Rottweiler she had ever seen walked right up to her in the living room, tail wagging.

"Goddamn," Kaitlyn said. "That's a big fucking dog." She extended a fist, which the Rottweiler sniffed, and then licked.

"His name is Victor," Tina said. "And he's basically my dog, now."

"No, he's not," Leo said. "Victor still belongs to me and Jinx."

Who the fuck is Jinx? Kaitlyn wondered.

As if reading her mind, DeVonte shot her a look. "Jinx is my brother. He's not home right now."

"Come on," Tina told her. "Let's go hang out in my room."

As Kaitlyn followed her up to the second floor, Victor followed them both up the stairs.

In Tina's room, Kaitlyn set her suitcase on the floor. Tina closed the door and locked it. Victor plopped down on the floor next to the bed and started gnawing on a rawhide bone.

Tina opened one of her bottles of whiskey. "What's in your suitcase?"

"Clothes and books, mostly," Kaitlyn said.

"Ah, so you like to read?"

"Yes, I love to read."

"Me too." Tina took a drink. "Reading is one of my favorite pleasures." She then sat down on the bed, putting her back against the headboard, and patted the queen-sized mattress. "You can come and sit next to me. I don't bite."

Kaitlyn joined her on the bed, putting her back against the headboard, too. "I'm ready for a drink of that whiskey."

Tina handed her the bottle. Kaitlyn took a drink and gave the bottle back.

From her nightstand, Tina grabbed a remote control and turned her TV on. "For background noise," she explained. "Unless there's something you wanna watch."

Kaitlyn shook her head. "I never watch TV."

Tina set the remote down. "Me neither."

They passed the bottle back and forth while a hip-hop video played on one of the music channels.

"I hate modern rap," Tina said. "I like old-school hip-hop: Tupac, Biggie, Jay-Z, Eminem, DMX."

"Same here. What kind of books do you like to read?"

Tina shrugged. "Just whatever. But mostly horror fiction."

"Same! I love horror fiction! Although I'm currently reading a nonfiction book called *Savage Messiah.*"

"*Savage Messiah?*"

"Yeah. It's about a Canadian doomsday cult called the Ant Hill Kids."

Tina took a drink. "Never heard of them."

"Most people haven't. The Ant Hill Kids were formed by a maniac named Roch Thériault in 1977. He claimed to be a prophet, called himself Moses, and formed the cult to save himself and his followers from a coming apocalypse."

"Let me guess: he fucked all the women and molested all the kids."

"Of course," Kaitlyn said. "But it got much worse than that. He was a heavy drinker, and his rules became stricter and stricter, until eventually his followers weren't even allowed to speak to each other unless he was present. If a person tried to leave, he would beat them with a hammer, or hang them from a ceiling and pluck out each and every hair on their body, or cut them with knives and have other members defecate on them."

"Damn," Tina said. "That's fucking brutal."

"Yes, and his punishments became more and more severe. He made the cult members sit on lit stoves, or shoot each other in the shoulders, or break their own legs with sledgehammers. He would forcibly remove their teeth, make them eat dead mice and feces, and cut off their arms and legs without warning. He would strip them naked, drag them outside into the freezing cold, and beat them with belts and whips. He often held children over fires, or nailed them to trees and made other children throw stones at them. He also made his followers cut off other followers' toes with wire cutters to prove their loyalty."

"And this is all true?"

"Yes. You can look it up. A doomsday cult called the Ant Hill Kids."

Tina took a drink. "How have I never heard of this?"

"No idea. But check this out: he also got drunk and performed surgeries on his followers."

"Surgeries?"

"Yes. A person would be held down, fully conscious, by other followers, and Thériault would go to work on them with pliers, a blowtorch, or whatever kitchen utensils were available. Most of the people lost teeth, fingers, toes, and entire limbs to his surgical techniques. Let me hit that whiskey."

Tina handed her the bottle. Kaitlyn took a drink and gave the bottle back.

"There was one woman," Kaitlyn said, "who complained of stomach pain, so Thériault stripped her naked, laid her on the kitchen table, punched her in the stomach, and shoved a tube up her ass to perform an enema with olive oil. Then he cut open her abdomen, ripped out pieces of her intestines with his bare hands, and forced another member to stitch her up. He shoved another tube down her throat and made the other women blow air into it. The woman died, of course, but Thériault—claiming the power of resurrection—drilled a hole into her skull and made the male followers ejaculate into her brain. When she didn't come back to life, they buried her corpse not far from the compound."

Tina took a drink. "How did he get caught?"

Kaitlyn shrugged. "I'm not exactly sure. I haven't finished the book yet, but I think one of the women escaped and turned him in. I *do* know that he ended up dying in prison. One of the inmates stabbed him in the neck. Can we get high now?"

"Of course. I have cocaine, OxyContin, crystal meth—"

"Let's do some coke," Kaitlyn said.

They did, snorting lines off a compact mirror on the bed through a clipped straw.

Afterward, Tina said, "Now I'm in the mood for love. Do you like girls?"

"I do. And I'm in the mood for you."

They kissed and began removing each other's clothes.

Chapter 22

"We should take a road trip," Roxanne said, lying next to Jinx on her bed.

He closed his book and looked over at her. "A road trip?"

"Yes. All we do is get drunk and fuck. A road trip would give us a chance to get to know each other."

Jinx lit a cigarette. "I'll be taking a road trip soon, but it's gonna be work-related, so I can't leave now, because I'm waiting for someone to call me and tell me to hit the road."

"Ah, okay. Never mind."

"Why? Where did you wanna go, anyway?"

Roxanne sipped her drink. "I wanna go see my father in Casper, Wyoming. I was gonna drive, if you wanted to go, but since you don't, I'll just take a plane instead."

Jinx nodded. "Cool. I'll go home and check in with Leo, Tina, and DeVonte. I hope you have a good time with your father."

"He's not really my father," Roxanne said. "My real father died overseas."

"In a war?"

"Yes. I never knew him. Then my mother married Don Hargrove when I was young, so he became my stepdad, and they gave me his last name. My mom died not long after that."

"I'm sorry to hear that," Jinx said. "How did she die?"

"She was struck by lightning."

"Damn."

"I know, right? Anyway, after that, my stepfather started . . . well, let's just say that he wasn't very nice to me. He and I have some unresolved issues."

In the ashtray between them, Jinx stubbed out his cigarette. "Maybe you'll get those issues resolved."

Roxanne finished her drink. "If you see Tina, tell her I said hello."

Chapter 23

In Casper, Wyoming, on a winding two-lane road, Christina handled the car with a skill Ashley admired.

"You're such a good driver," Ashley said.

Christina grinned. "Thanks! And you're good at *everything* you do."

Ashley put a hand on Christina's leg. "I'm looking forward to spending the weekend with you."

On their way to the campground, Christina stopped at a camping-supplies store. She parked near the front, and they went inside.

Ashley looked around. "This place is huge."

The interior—cavernous—was filled with more hunting rifles and compact bows than Ashley had ever seen.

Christina used her bankcard to purchase two sleeping bags, a fast-pitch tent, a can of lighter fluid, and a four-pack bundle of campfire roasting logs.

"Want me to give you some cash?" Ashley said. "To pay for half?"

Christina shook her head. "Nah, but you can buy the beer when I stop for gas."

At a gas station, while Christina filled the tank, Ashley went inside to get some beer. They already had food and water in the car, but she went ahead and purchased several snacks.

Soon thereafter, they arrived at the campground and checked in. Christina parked her car near their assigned campsite, and they got out.

Ashley looked around. Spruce trees surrounded the clearing on which they stood. To the west, the sun had begun lowering over the mountains.

Ashley drank a beer while Christina set up the tent. They dragged their sleeping bags into the tent and made love. Then they took a nap, woke up, and made love again.

Darkness descended. They got a fire going and roasted marshmallows beneath the stars. After they ate, they drank beer, smoked cigarettes, and told each other ghost stories.

Then Christina leaned her head on Ashley's shoulder.

"Are you tired?" Ashley said.

Christina shrugged. "I don't know. I think I just have a buzz."

Ashley kissed the top of her head. "Me too."

As she stared into the flames, the heat of the fire felt good on Ashley's face. She looked up into the sky and saw sparks rising toward the stars. Then she heard a noise and turned toward it.

A man had joined them by the fire. He appeared to be in his fifties. "It's a beautiful night for camping," he said.

Then he raised a silencer-fitted pistol and shot Christina once through the head, killing her instantly.

Before Ashley could even scream, the man bashed her alongside the head with his gun—then all she saw was darkness.

***

She woke up naked on a chair in what looked like a basement. Moonlight spilling through an old, crank-style window above her head illuminated the room.

Ashley tried to get up but failed, then realized she was not merely sitting on the chair—she was tied to it. Ropes bound her chest and waist, and more ropes were tied across her thighs, securing her to the seat. Her arms were fastened to the arms of the chair below her elbows and again at her wrists.

She still had a slight beer buzz, but—other than a major headache from the man clubbing her with his gun—her mind felt clear, and she vividly remembered him blowing Christina's brains out with his pistol.

Tears filled Ashley's eyes as the reality set in that never again would she hear Christina laugh. Never again would they make love nor hold each other afterward while talking about their plans for the future. She would never again look into Christina's eyes nor run her fingers through her beautiful hair.

Ashley heard a door open behind her. Moments later, someone turned on a light.

Then the man entered her field of vision. He held a claw hammer in one hand and a butcher's knife in the other.

"I'm glad you're awake," he told her. Then he slid a footstool in front of her chair and sat down.

"Why are you doing this to me?" Ashley said.

He smiled. "I haven't even done anything yet. But I'm going to, of course. Oh yes, I'm going to do a lot of bad things to you."

"But why?" Ashley repeated. "Why are you doing this to me?"

He shrugged. "I don't know. This is just what I do."

Still holding the claw hammer, he set the butcher's knife on the floor and withdrew what looked like a driver's license from his back pocket. "Ashley Malvern," he said. "And I see that you're twenty-two years old."

He spun the card around, and Ashley saw that it was not a driver's license: it was her underground-coal-miner-apprentice certification that she had received from the Mine Safety and Health Administration.

He returned the card to his back pocket. "Underground coal mining. Dangerous work."

"I haven't started yet," Ashley said. "I'm supposed to start on Monday. Christina and I wanted to spend the weekend together, before I started my new job. And then you killed her."

The man raised the claw hammer. "I used to be a coal miner, a long time ago. For a few years, anyway. But I don't remember seeing any women in the mines back then. Hell, there's probably not many, now. It's a shitty fucking job, though. I can tell you that much. You won't be missing anything."

Then he swung the hammer down onto the concrete floor, missing her left foot by an inch, and Ashley screamed.

The man laughed. "I'm tempted to smash your toes and your feet to smithereens, but I'm not gonna torture you right now. Not yet, anyway. Right now, I'm just gonna let you sit here and percolate for a while, let you think about all the things I'm gonna do to you."

Rising from the footstool, he spat into her face. "I don't have any neighbors, by the way, so you can scream and yell all you want."

The man walked away. Moments later, he turned off the light.

Ashley heard him slam the door behind her. Then she heard him stomping up a set of stairs, leaving her alone in the dark.

***

At two in the morning, Don Hargrove stood before a frying pan on the stove in his kitchen. Green peppers, mushrooms, and onions sizzled in the pan. Using a fillet knife, he cut strips of meat from a thawed chicken breast and tossed them into the dish, which would be Ashley's final meal before he tortured her to death. Then he covered the pan with a lid and washed his hands.

While drying his hands with a dishrag at the kitchen sink, he heard a woman behind him say, "New Daddy. Long time no see."

Don Hargrove spun around and saw his stepdaughter, Roxanne, pointing a silencer-fitted pistol at his chest. She stood six feet away, with the hand not holding the gun gripping the strap of a duffel bag hanging from her shoulder. He had not seen her in years, but recognized her immediately, for he had followed her career on social media, and he knew that Roxanne was a highly successful horror novelist.

"How did you get in here?" he said.

Roxanne smiled. "I have my ways."

He nodded, and then pointed toward the frying pan. "I'm making some chicken stir fry. Would you like some?"

Before Roxanne could answer, the woman tied up in Don's basement yelled, "Hey! Can you hear me up there? I'm thirsty! Will you bring me something to drink?"

Roxanne cocked her head. "Who the fuck is that?"

"Just a friend," Don said. "Her name is Ashley."

With the hand not pointing the pistol at his chest, Roxanne produced what looked like a toy gun from her duffel bag—but then Don realized it was a taser, which he found encouraging: perhaps she didn't intend to kill him, after all.

Then Roxanne shot him with the taser. Don felt his muscles freeze before he hit the floor. He never lost consciousness, however, as he watched his stepdaughter approach him with a hypodermic syringe.

Then she shoved the needle into his neck and pressed the plunger. Seconds later, he lost consciousness.

***

Behind Ashley, the door opened. Then the light came on. A woman entered her field of vision, raising a glass of yellow liquid to Ashley's lips.

"Apple juice," the woman told her.

Ashley drank. "Thank you," she said, after the glass was empty. "The man who lives here killed my girlfriend. Then he brought me down here and tied me up. Will you cut me loose?"

"I'll be right back," the woman said. "I'm gonna go get a knife."

***

Don Hargrove woke up on his kitchen floor. Roxanne loomed over him, aiming the silencer-fitted pistol at his face.

"I was going to chain you up," she told him. "I have a chain and some handcuffs in my duffel bag, along with some knives, pliers, and a blowtorch. I was gonna torture you to death for turning me into the monster I am today. But then I saw that woman in your basement and changed my mind. You're not even worth it. I don't feel like listening to you scream."

"So you're gonna let me live?"

Roxanne shook her head. "Of course not."

She pulled the trigger.

***

Behind Ashley, the door opened again. Then the woman entered her field of vision, holding a knife. "Thanks so much for cutting me loose," Ashley said.

The woman brought the knife to Ashley's face. "I'm not gonna cut you loose. Instead, I'm gonna finish what my stepfather started."

Ashley cocked her head. "What are you talking about?"

Pressing the blade to Ashley's cheek, the woman yanked it down.

Ashley screamed as the longest part of her final night began.

***

Later, during the flight back to Los Angeles, Roxanne sent a text message to Jinx: *I'm headed back to L.A. now. Are you still in town?*

He replied moments later: *Yep, I'm still here.*

Okay. Just checking. I thought maybe your employers had contacted you and told you to hit the road.

Nope, not yet. Want me to pick you up at the airport?

Sure. That would be great. I'll message you when I get there.

Cool, Jinx wrote. *I'm looking forward to seeing you.*

Chapter 24

Kaitlyn shuddered as Tina brushed fingertips across her upper thigh.

"I hope you know I'm already in love with you, Kaitlyn."

They lay naked on the bed in Tina's room, after making love all night, and now the rising sun cast beams of golden light through the bedroom window.

"You are?"

"Yes," Tina said. "I'm already madly in love with you."

Kaitlyn kissed her on the lips. "Good, because I'm already in love with you, too."

They took a shower together.

Afterward, as they got dressed, Victor lay on the floor at the foot of the bed, gnawing on a rawhide bone. When they headed down to the first floor, the Rottweiler followed them down the stairs.

***

In the living room, DeVonte sat on the loveseat, drinking whiskey. Leo sat to his left, cleaning a disassembled pistol on the sofa. The grip of another pistol was visible in the shoulder rig he wore.

The TV was on, but DeVonte was barely listening. Setting his bottle on the coffee table, he lit a cigarette.

Moments later, Tina, Kaitlyn, and the Rottweiler came downstairs. As they crossed the living room, DeVonte said, "Do y'all need a ride somewhere?"

"No thanks," Tina said. "We're gonna take Victor for a walk down to the cemetery."

They left.

DeVonte took a drink, and then Leo told him, "I saw the way you were looking at Kaitlyn."

DeVonte shrugged. "She's very attractive."

"Whatever," Leo said. "You're a necrophiliac, dude. She'd have to drop dead before you'd touch her."

Not true, DeVonte thought. *I could always kill the bitch myself.*

Chapter 25

In downtown Los Angeles, in her bedroom on the fifth floor of a seven-story building she owned, Xayla stood sipping bourbon-spiked tea in a black robe when her phone chimed. She checked the message.

As expected, Larry North—downstairs in the nightclub on the first floor—informed her that Wilson Blendin, a billionaire from New York, had arrived.

"Send him up," Xayla said. Then she stepped out into the hallway.

Moments later, Wilson Blendin—without Larry North—stepped out of an elevator and joined her in the hall. He wore an Armani suit, and his face was remarkably fresh for a man of eighty-two. Xayla suspected he had spent a fortune on cosmetic surgery.

"Good evening, Mister Blendin. It's good to see you again."

He nodded, holding a briefcase. "It's good to see you too, Xayla. And please, call me Wilson."

She smiled. "As you wish. Shall we step into my room?"

"Of course."

She led him into her suite, where he set his briefcase on her bed and opened it, revealing banded stacks of currency within.

"It's all there," Wilson said. "You can count it, if you'd like."

Xayla shook her head. "That's okay. I'll be right back with your groceries."

Using a key, she unlocked a closet door, opened it, and walked inside, closing the door behind her and locking it. She then released a trapdoor ladder in the ceiling and climbed onto the sixth floor of the building, emerging near the center of a vast, windowless chamber.

A few rooms had been sectioned off during the construction of this level, but the majority of the sixth floor was open space, like a warehouse. The smell up here was terrible, despite the ventilation systems, but nothing could be done about that.

American citizens—men, women, and children—were chained to poles that ran from the floor to the ceiling throughout the dimly-lit expanse. All were gagged, and each had a bucket in which to deposit bodily wastes. Perhaps a hundred captives were imprisoned up here at any given time, brought in from all over America.

This was not only Xayla's own personal torture chamber (where she came to inflict pain and death upon the Americans), but also a place where sadistic millionaires and billionaires could, for a fee, torture American citizens to death. The minimal rooms were soundproof—as was the entire building—and equipped with operating tables, sex toys, oxyacetylene torches, hammers, knives, and all manner of surgical instruments.

And every member of the ITB (International Terrorist Brotherhood) who came and went down on the fourth floor was brought up here at least once to torture, rape, and kill an American before being sent away on assignment.

Xayla strolled past gagged captives, ignoring their muffled pleas, and retrieved Wilson's groceries from a temperature-controlled, cryonic room. She carried the steel container of frozen fetuses down the ladder in her closet. Leaving the trapdoor open (she intended to torture an American to death before she went to sleep), she carried the steel container out of the closet and locked the door behind her.

Wilson Blendin stood where she had left him, at the foot of her bed.

"Dinner is served," Xayla said. "Or many dinners, rather." She placed the steel container on the floor within his reach.

"Wet or dry ice?" Wilson inquired.

Xayla smiled. "Liquid nitrogen."

"And all of the fetuses are intact?"

"Absolutely. They were all aborted right before birth. There's not a fetus in that container who was snatched at less than thirty-three weeks gestation. Feel free to open it and conduct an examination."

Wilson shook his head. "Nah, that's okay. I trust you. Besides, I need to keep them in suspension until I put them in my own cryogenic freezer in New York. It's been a pleasure doing business with you."

"Likewise."

He lifted the steel container. "I'll be calling you soon. These fetuses—when thawed and consumed—do miracles for self-rejuvenation."

Xayla nodded. "They certainly do."

She escorted him out into the hallway, where he got back in the elevator and descended, then Xayla returned to her suite.

She finished her bourbon-spiked tea and mixed another one, for she would need something to drink while torturing an American upstairs.

She was halfway to the closet when someone knocked on her door.

Setting her glass down, Xayla grabbed a pistol off the coffee table. Then she crossed the room and opened the door.

Larry North—the only American she employed—stood before her. "I'm sorry to bother you," he said. "I sent you another message, but you didn't respond."

Xayla lowered her gun. "I turned my volume off. I wasn't expecting any more calls."

"I see. Well, again, I'm sorry to bother you, but that gentleman from Birmingham arrived unannounced."

"Oliver Burgess?"

"Yes, the necrophiliac. He's downstairs in the club. I scolded him for not making an appointment, but he's desperate, says the need is urgent, and brought full payment in cash. Would you like me to turn him away, or send him up?"

"Send him up."

While Larry made a phone call, Xayla stepped out of her suite and closed the door. Minutes later, the necrophiliac joined them in the hall. Oliver Burgess held a briefcase, and he had gained a few pounds since the last time Xayla saw him.

She pulled a blindfold from a pocket in her robe and handed it to him. "You know the drill."

Oliver set the briefcase on the floor and put the blindfold on.

Xayla, still holding the gun, used her left hand to pick up the briefcase. Then she followed Larry as he guided Oliver to a private elevator down the hall.

Moments later, all three emerged on the sixth floor.

Some of the gagged captives chained to poles wept and implored them with their eyes. The foul air reeked of excrement, urine, and body odor.

Oliver—still blindfolded—took a deep breath through his nose. "Ah, it smells wonderful in here."

A few of the captives with the strength to move reached for them as Xayla followed Larry and Oliver into a small, windowless room used for torture and closed the door. The room featured a four-poster bed.

Pointing the gun at Oliver, Xayla said, "You can take the blindfold off now."

Oliver pulled the blindfold off his head.

Xayla lowered the gun. "Let me guess: a woman no older than thirty."

"Yes," Oliver said.

"A thin woman with firm breasts?"

"Yes, but not too big. I don't like overly-large tits. And make sure she has long hair."

"Any color preference?"

"No, I don't care. Just make sure it's long."

Xayla nodded. Then she set the briefcase on the floor. "Be right back."

Leaving Oliver with Larry North, Xayla left the room and closed the door.

There were currently over a hundred Americans in chains on the sixth floor, and it didn't take her long to select a thin woman in her mid-twenties with firm breasts and long hair. Fetching some keys from a pocket in her robe, Xayla unchained her, grabbed her by the throat, and put the gun to her head. The woman's eyes widened with fear. Xayla did not ungag her, nor did she say anything to the woman. She simply dragged her—naked and whimpering—to the room in which Larry and the necrophiliac awaited.

Kicking the door shut behind her, Xayla tossed the woman onto the bed's plastic-covered mattress. "She's all yours."

Oliver glared down at the woman on the bed, who covered her breasts with her hands and curled up as if to make herself smaller.

Xayla asked Oliver, "Do you approve?"

He scratched his balding head. "Yes. She's beautiful. But she's . . . she's so . . . she's still *alive.*"

Xayla laughed. "You're spineless. You know that, right? You love to fuck corpses, and yet you lack the guts to commit cold-blooded murder."

She then looked at Larry North, and nodded.

Larry approached the woman on the bed. Grabbing her head with both hands, he twisted it to the left and broke her neck, killing her instantly.

"There you go," Xayla told Oliver. "She's dead now. How long will you need the corpse?"

"All night long. Same as always."

Xayla picked the briefcase up. "Once I lock you in this room, I won't be back to let you out until tomorrow."

Oliver smiled. "That's perfectly fine."

Xayla followed Larry out of the room and locked the door.

"Not so fast," she told him, as he headed toward the private elevator.

He stopped, turned around, and saw her pointing the gun at his chest. "What's the problem?"

"I saw something on the news earlier that piqued my interest," Xayla said. "A report about a pair of horribly-deformed female twins wanted for a string of homicides. Have you heard about them?"

Larry shook his head, staring into the gun's muzzle instead of Xayla's eyes. "Nope, sure haven't."

"The twins are seventeen, and they've been on a killing spree after breaking out of a psych ward in Jacksonville. They're believed to still be somewhere in the southeast, possibly heading to Texas to cross the border into Mexico."

Larry raised his gaze to meet her stare. "What does this have to do with me?"

"It means you didn't follow my orders seven years ago," Xayla said.

Larry cocked his head. "What are you talking about?"

"When I saw their faces on TV, I recognized them immediately. The twins haven't changed much in seven years, that's for damned sure: oversized, misshapen heads; bulbous eyes; crowded, malformed teeth. They're still as hideous as they've always been. Perhaps you remember their mother, Geisha Dupree."

"Of course. The hermaphrodite. She used to work for you in Atlanta."

Xayla laughed. "I believe the correct term these days is *intersex person,* but yes, the hermaphrodite. She claimed to have impregnated herself and to have given birth to twins, even though most say that's impossible."

"Deus unicus creatus," Larry said.

"Is that Latin?"

"Yes. God's unique creation."

Setting the briefcase on the floor, Xayla aimed her gun at Larry's face. "Seven years ago, after Geisha double-crossed me in Atlanta, I told you to bring me her head in a box, and you did. But I also told you to kill her daughters first, and to make her watch, and you *told* me you did, but you did not, because they're still alive, and now they're wanted by the FBI for a string of homicides. So you lied to me, and I'm pretty sure I know why."

Larry cocked his head again. "You do?"

"Yes. You lied because you like little girls. The twins are seventeen now, which is much too old for you, but back then they were ten, and you were fucking them—even though they're hideous in appearance."

Larry nodded. "I was in love, and I couldn't kill them. Despite their horrible deformities, I was madly in love with them both. So I pulled some strings and hid them in a psych ward in Jacksonville. Are you gonna kill me?"

"No." Xayla lowered the gun. "Love will make you do some crazy things, so I'll pardon your disobedience, but just this once. Something like this can never happen again. Do you understand me?"

"Yes, one hundred percent."

"Good." Xayla looked around at some of the captives. "Now I'm going to torture someone to death. Would you like to join me?"

He smiled. "I would love to."

She withdrew her keys. "I'll let you pick. Man, woman, or child?"

"Child," Larry said. "A little girl."

She gave him the keys. "I knew you were going to say that."

He selected a young girl with pigtails and unchained her. Then he dragged her into a room that featured an operating table surrounded by surgical instruments.

Lifting the briefcase off the floor, Xayla followed Larry into the room and closed the door.

Chapter 26

"Seriously?" Kaitlyn said, interrupting Tina's story. "Cannibal politicians in Washington, D.C.?"

Tina took a drink. "Yep. The whole thing was surreal."

They sat beneath a tree in the cemetery, passing a bottle of whiskey back and forth. To their left, Victor lay on the ground, gnawing on a rawhide bone. The day was warm. The sky was blue. The sun had begun lowering to the west.

"What were you doing in a psychiatrist's basement?" Kaitlyn said.

Tina shrugged. "I was tied up with rope to an old radiator. I had only been seeing him to get meds for my mental disorders, but it turned out the doctor was even crazier than I am. He killed my parents, abducted me, and kept me tied up in his basement."

"And this was in Virginia?"

"Yep. When Jinx and Leo showed up at his house to get drugs on their way to D.C., they heard me screaming down in the basement."

"So they killed the doctor?"

"Yeah, but that had nothing to do with me. They only came downstairs to see who I was. After they cut me loose, I asked them if I could go with them, because I had nowhere else to go, and they said yes. Then we all three took off in their tour bus."

"Tour bus?"

"Yes." Tina pointed to the Rottweiler. "It's where I first met Victor. He was guarding the hostages chained to poles inside the bus—all the people that Jinx and Leo had abducted from the highways while traveling east. When we got to D.C., they took the people to the cannibals in a warehouse downtown."

"The cannibal politicians?"

"Yes. The politicians were having a dinner party inside the warehouse—with the hostages as the main course. But the warehouse only looked like a warehouse from the outside. Once you got inside, it was a huge red ballroom, with men in white tuxedos and women in white dresses and ball gowns."

"So they actually took you inside with them?"

"Yep. They even introduced me to their boss—some creepy dude they called Senator Fox. The whole thing was crazy."

"Sounds like it," Kaitlyn said. "Let me hit that whiskey."

Tina handed her the bottle. Kaitlyn took a drink and gave the bottle back.

They drank until the bottle was empty, then walked Victor back up to Jinx and Leo's compound at the top of the hill.

In the driveway, Kaitlyn pointed toward the barn. "Is that where they keep the tour bus?"

"Yes," Tina said. She then pointed to a black Cadillac in front of the main house that Kaitlyn had never seen. "And Jinx is home, by the way, so you'll finally get to meet him."

On the front porch, before they entered the house, the front door opened. Then a tall, skinny black man whom Kaitlyn had never seen stepped outside.

"Speak of the devil," Tina said. "Jinx, this is my new girlfriend, Kaitlyn."

He flashed her a smile. "It's nice to meet you."

Kaitlyn returned his smile. "It's nice to meet you, too."

"Are you leaving?" Tina asked him.

"Yep." He reached down to rub Victor's massive head. "I gotta go pick Roxanne up at the airport."

Tina nodded. "Cool. Tell her I said hello."

"Will do," Jinx said. He then headed toward the Cadillac.

Kaitlyn followed Tina inside the house.

In the living room, Leo sat on the sofa, watching TV, drinking a beer, and smoking a cigarette. DeVonte sat on the loveseat, clutching a bottle of whiskey. He glared at Kaitlyn, but didn't say anything.

Kaitlyn followed Tina upstairs into her room.

"So," Tina said, "what did you think of Jinx?"

Kaitlyn shrugged. "I don't know, but DeVonte gives me the fucking creeps."

Chapter 27

The plane landed at LAX, and Roxanne disembarked. She sent a text to Jinx: *Just got off the plane. How long will you be?*

He replied almost immediately: *I'm already here, on the top level. I'll pick you up at the curb in front of the terminal.*

Soon thereafter, she climbed into his Cadillac on the passenger's side.

From World Way out of the airport, Jinx took West Century to South Sepulveda, and they headed north.

"I'm hungry," Roxanne said. "Can we stop at a restaurant?"

Jinx parked at a restaurant in Inglewood. They got out and went inside.

Ten minutes later, while cutting into the filet mignon on her plate, Roxanne said, "Still no word from your employers?"

"No," Jinx told her. "And I'm worried about my brother."

"DeVonte?"

"Yes."

"What about him?"

Jinx swallowed a piece of his grilled chicken. "Well," he said, looking around the restaurant, "DeVonte's always been crazy, but now he seems crazier than ever." Then he looked at Roxanne and lowered his voice. "You know he only fucks dead chicks, right?"

She nodded. "Yeah, you've mentioned it."

Jinx sipped his cola. "I don't think he's been laid in a while, and I think that's part of his problem. And if our bosses call, and Leo and I have to leave town, I'm afraid DeVonte might go on a killing spree. And I'd hate to see my brother get in trouble. Know what I mean?"

"I can help your brother with his problem," Roxanne said.

Jinx cocked his head. "How? You know somebody who works in a morgue, or some shit?"

Roxanne cracked a grin. "No, but I have an ex-girlfriend, Xayla—with whom I'm still friends, by the way—who makes those cannibal politicians you work for seem kinda tame."

"Is that so?"

"Yes. She runs a place here in L.A. where people can spend money to satisfy the darkest desires in their souls. At Xayla's place, DeVonte can kill as many women as he likes."

Finished with his food, Jinx shoved his plate to the edge of the table for the waitress.

"Text your brother," Roxanne told him. "Give him my address and tell him to meet us there in about an hour."

Chapter 28

In the living room, DeVonte sat on the loveseat, drinking whiskey. To his left, Leo sat on the sofa, drinking beer and watching an old sitcom on TV. Every time Leo laughed, DeVonte resisted an urge to pull the pistol from the waistband of his jeans and blow the white dude's brains out the back of his skull.

Instead, DeVonte stared at the bottle he held and thought about his parents, who were dead and gone—which was all to the good, in his opinion. At least they weren't around to express concerns about his mental instability, having deduced during his childhood that their son had become unhinged.

"Not irrevocably so," his mother had often told him, "but certainly enough to warrant professional intervention."

"Your mother and I," his father had often said, "would like for you to go see a psychiatrist."

Fuck you both, DeVonte thought. *I hope you burn in Hell through all eternity.*

To his left, Leo's phone chimed on the coffee table, and Leo reached for it.

"That might be Senator Fox," Leo said. He checked his phone. "Nope. It's your brother. He wants you to check your messages."

DeVonte shot him a look. "What are you talking about?"

"I'm talking about your brother, dude—Jinx. He wants you to check your messages. He knows you keep the volume on your phone off."

Setting his bottle down, DeVonte checked his phone. "He sent me Roxanne Hargrove's address. He wants me to meet them at her mansion in the Santa Monica Mountains. You wanna go with me?"

Leo shook his head. "Nah, dude. I'm just gonna chill out here. Might order some food."

"Cool," DeVonte said.

He took the bottle with him when he left.

Chapter 29

"I'm wasted," Kaitlyn said, lying next to Tina on the bed.

"Me too. I say we take a nap."

"Sounds like a great idea."

After watching Kaitlyn close her eyes, Tina closed her own. The last thing she heard was Victor on the floor, gnawing on a rawhide bone at the foot of the bed.

***

Tina opened her eyes. Beyond the bedroom window, night had fallen. Kaitlyn sat up next to her on the bed.

"I had the craziest dream," Kaitlyn said.

"I gotta brush my teeth. I'll be right back." Tina got up, brushed her teeth in the adjoining bathroom, and then returned to the bedroom. "Do you like vodka? I'm in the mood for something other than whiskey."

Kaitlyn nodded. "I love vodka."

From beneath the bed, Tina retrieved a bottle of vodka and cracked it open.

"You people never run out of booze in this house, do you?" Kaitlyn said.

Tina shook her head. "Never." She took a drink. "Tell me about your dream."

"Okay. In the dream, you and I were in this massive library, and no one else was there. Just you and me. But I can't even describe how big this library was. It was like its own fucking planet of books, or some shit. I mean, the ceiling was so high above us that we could barely see it, and the bookshelves extended for miles and miles in all directions, for as far as we could see."

"That sounds like paradise to me," Tina said.

"Yeah, it seemed that way to me, too—at first. Then we came upon this bookcase of Cormac McCarthy novels."

Tina took a drink. "One of our favorite authors."

"Yes. Let me hit that vodka."

Tina handed her the bottle. Kaitlyn took a drink and gave the bottle back.

"Anyway," Kaitlyn went on, "at the Cormac McCarthy bookcase, we each selected one of his books to read again. You selected *Outer Dark,* and I selected *Child of God,* and then we ended up stumbling into this skating rink."

"Skating rink?"

"Yes, like a roller-skating rink. It was huge, and no one else was in there. So you and I walked out to the middle of the rink and sat down to read our books, but then these children came from out of nowhere all at once and surrounded us along the rink's perimeter."

"Children?"

"Yes, little boys and girls, all of them maybe seven or eight years old. And they all wore these black-and-white uniforms, like kids in a Catholic school, or something. They started laughing, pointing at us, and teasing us for reading, telling us that no one reads anymore. Then this huge white dude stepped out of the shadows and told the kids to get back to his classroom."

"Did they leave?"

"Yes, they vanished. They immediately just disappeared from view. And the white dude was *huge*. I'm talking seven feet tall, at least, with long black hair pulled back in a ponytail. He stood about a hundred feet away from us, but he had this booming voice that carried across the skating rink."

"What did he say?"

"He started talking about names, first, and how important they are. And he knew our names, by the way. He called you Tina, and he called me Kaitlyn. He told us that he inhabited many forms, and that this was just the form he had currently chosen. Then he told us that he had many names, and that you and I should call him The Disk Thrower."

"The Disk Thrower?"

"Yes. He even spelled it out for us, like we were kids in his classroom. He told us to use the letter *k* at the end of disk instead of *c*. For some reason, he wanted us to know that. Then he recited that old sticks-and-stones nursery rhyme."

"Sticks and stones?"

"Yeah. You know the one. Sticks and stones may break my bones, but words will never hurt me?"

Tina took a drink. "Of course."

"He told us that it's not true, that words can be the most hurtful weapons of all. Then he said, 'Here, you'll see what I mean.' Then he threw a silver disk at me."

"A silver disk?"

"Yeah, it looked like a silver frisbee. And I caught it like a frisbee, too. It was ice-cold, and it felt like metal, but it wasn't heavy. I didn't even know it had cut me until you told me I was bleeding."

"It cut you? When you caught it?"

"Yeah, but it wasn't bad. It was like a papercut, I guess. Then he threw a disk at you, and it cut you, too. But you had to catch it. If you hadn't caught it, it would have hit you in the face."

Tina took a drink. "That's crazy."

"Yeah. Let me hit that vodka."

Tina handed her the bottle. Kaitlyn took a drink and gave the bottle back.

"Anyway," Kaitlyn went on, "we're standing there bleeding, holding the disks, and then he starts throwing more disks at us. And we don't wanna catch them, of course, so we use the disks we're holding to block the incoming disks. But they start coming faster, and faster, and faster, and we can't block them all. We start getting cuts all over our bodies, so we take off running, still under fire. I mean, those disks are lighting us up like a swarm of bees. And The

Disk Thrower's laughing the entire time, screaming, "NOW DO YOU SEE WHAT I MEAN? WORDS ARE WEAPONS! NOW DO YOU SEE WHAT I MEAN?"

"Jesus fucking Christ," Tina said. "Then what happened?"

"We made it out of the skating rink, but by then, it was too late. We were basically already dead—we just didn't know it. We stumbled into this room of mirrors, and screamed at each other's skulls in our reflections. Our faces were gone. There was nothing left of our faces but a few scraps of flesh hanging from our skulls. Same with our bodies. We were basically skeletons. All of our clothes and most of our flesh had been sliced away. And then I woke up."

"Crazy dream," Tina said, rising from the bed. "Wanna go drink this bottle in the cemetery?"

Kaitlyn got up and grabbed her shoes. "Let's do it."

Tina grabbed a fresh rawhide bone from her dresser. "Come on, Victor. We're going for a walk."

Rising from the floor, the Rottweiler stretched and followed them down the stairs.

Chapter 30

After keying the address Jinx gave him into the Maps app on his phone, DeVonte wept while driving to Roxanne's mansion in the Santa Monica Mountains, occasionally drinking from the bottle of whiskey on the passenger's seat. A box of tissues sat next to the bottle, and he kept a plastic bag on the floorboard in which to put his trash.

He knew he often became too emotional when he got drunk, but tonight, it was not the booze that made him cry. *I'm empty,* he thought. *Absolutely depleted. And I don't think I'll ever be filled again.*

DeVonte turned the radio on, but then quickly turned it off, wondering if he had ever been filled in the first place. Probably not. Then he wondered: *have I ever been happy?* The more he thought about it, DeVonte found that he didn't believe in happiness. He figured the most a person could hope for was relative contentment—interspersed with periods of joy, perhaps—but nothing more. True happiness was a pipe dream; it simply didn't exist, not for him or anyone else. Sorrow, on the other hand, was as real as all the oceans on planet Earth, but deeper, for at least an ocean has a floor. Sorrows were bottomless, with each one leading deeper and deeper into miseries previously unimagined. Devonte found the whole thing sad.

According to the dashboard clock, the time was 10:06 p.m. when he arrived at Roxanne's estate. The gate at the bottom of her driveway was open, and he drove through.

At the top, numerous outdoor lanterns illuminated the manicured grounds, and the mansion was even bigger and more impressive than he'd expected. He parked his car behind Jinx's Cadillac in a circular drive near the main entrance and took a drink of whiskey.

Then he sent his brother a text: *I'm here.*

Cool, Jinx wrote back. *We'll meet you at the front door.*

DeVonte capped the bottle, electing to leave the whiskey in his car. Then he got out and approached the main entrance.

Moments later, Roxanne—whom DeVonte recognized from her author photos—opened the front door. Behind her stood Jinx, who towered over her. "DeVonte!" Jinx said, smiling. "It's good to see you, my brother. Come on in."

Roxanne stepped aside, permitting DeVonte's entry. "It's nice to meet you," she told him.

"It's nice to meet you, too."

DeVonte stepped inside. From the foyer, he followed them into the great room, where Roxanne asked him, "Would you like something to drink?"

"No thank you. But I *would* like to know why you have summoned me here."

Jinx pointed toward an armchair. "Have a seat."

DeVonte sat down, then Jinx and Roxanne sat down on a loveseat.

"I've been worried about you," Jinx told him. "You seem a little crazier than usual."

DeVonte wanted to break something. "Oh, so now you're calling me crazy?"

"Nah, brother. It ain't like that. But of course you're crazy. Hell, I'm crazy, Roxanne's crazy—everybody's crazy. But I don't wanna see you get in trouble."

DeVonte cocked his head. "What are you talking about?"

"Listen," Jinx said. "Leo and I are gonna be leaving town soon, and I don't wanna have to worry about you getting in trouble while I'm on the road, so Roxanne's gonna introduce you to one of her friends who can hook you up with the type of women you like."

"The type of women I like?"

"Yeah. You know . . . *dead* women."

DeVonte looked at Roxanne; she smiled at him.

Then he returned his gaze to Jinx. "Why the fuck you telling this bitch my business?"

"Whoa, slow down, bro," Jinx said. "Don't be calling my girl a bitch."

From his jacket's interior pocket, DeVonte drew his silencer-fitted pistol and aimed it at Jinx. "I'll be Cain," he said, "and you can go be Abel."

Jinx put a hand up. "Now wait a goddamn—"

DeVonte shot his brother between the eyes, killing him instantly.

Then he pointed the gun at Roxanne—who had not even flinched when Jinx's blood hit the side of her face. "I'm impressed," he told her. "You don't scare easily."

She shrugged, covered in his brother's blood. "I have watched many people die. It doesn't bother me."

Rising from the chair, DeVonte approached Roxanne and shoved the gun into her face. "What about your own death? Are you afraid of that?"

"No, for nothing has ever existed that the universe did not intend to kill."

DeVonte lowered the gun. "Fair enough."

He returned the gun to his jacket's interior pocket. Then he wrapped both hands around her throat and squeezed so hard he crushed her larynx.

She tried to fight back, but it was useless, for DeVonte was too strong. The sound of her trachea popping was music to his ears.

Eventually, her head flopped to one side and her eyes rolled back in her head. DeVonte continued squeezing long after he knew she was dead. Then he stripped her naked and removed his own clothes, but was unable to achieve an erection.

"It's all your fault," he told his brother's corpse, which still sat next to Roxanne's on the loveseat. "My dick won't get hard because your dick's already been inside her. But that's okay. I'll chop her head off and fuck her skull later. Hell, I'll chop your head off, too, and make you watch."

Still naked, DeVonte found some disposable gloves in the kitchen and put them on. Then he found some black trash bags, a carving knife, a meat cleaver, and returned to the great room.

He sawed off Roxanne's head first, and then his brother's. He put the heads in separate trash bags. Then he put the gloves in one of the trash bags, too. Afterward, he washed the blood off his chest and arms at the kitchen sink.

I'll take a shower later, he thought. *After I fuck Roxanne's skull.*

DeVonte got dressed. Then he grabbed the trash bags and left.

Chapter 31

"Midnight in the cemetery," Tina said. "My favorite time and my favorite place to be."

She and Kaitlyn sat beneath a tree, passing the bottle of vodka back and forth. Victor lay between them, gnawing on a rawhide bone.

"I'm still thinking about that dream," Kaitlyn said.

"About the Disk Thrower?"

"Yes."

Tina took a drink. "It's true what those kids told you in the dream, that no one reads books anymore."

"You and I read books," Kaitlyn said.

"I know. But we're the last of a dying breed. Most people would rather watch videos on their phones."

Kaitlyn looked at Tina, and smiled. "According to Cormac McCarthy, people who enjoy reading the same books share a force more binding than blood."

"That's us," Tina said. "And I'm so glad I found you. But I'm gonna miss Victor when he's gone."

Kaitlyn glanced at the Rottweiler. "Victor's leaving us?"

"He will be. Every time Leo and Jinx leave town, Victor has to leave, too."

"That's sad. I thought he was your dog, now."

"He is, basically. But he's still their guard dog. Victor guards the captives on the bus."

"The people they kidnap? For the cannibal politicians?"

"Yep. He's also an attack dog. Victor can kill on command. But that's not all he does. He can also chase, subdue, injure, amputate . . . all kinds of stuff."

"Damn. Do you know any of his commands?"

Tina nodded. "I know them all."

"Nice. Let me hit that vodka."

Tina handed her the bottle.

Kaitlyn took a drink and gave the bottle back. "I love you."

Tina leaned the bottle against a tombstone. Then she tapped two cigarettes from her pack and handed one to Kaitlyn. "I love you, too."

Chapter 32

In the living room, Leo sat on the sofa, drinking a beer and watching TV, when his phone rang. *Senator Fox?* he wondered, retrieving the phone from his pocket.

It was not Senator Fox. It was an unavailable number, and he didn't answer. *Probably a telemarketer,* he thought, setting his phone on the coffee table.

Moments later, he heard DeVonte's car pull up outside. Soon thereafter, DeVonte entered the living room holding a pair of trash bags.

"What the fuck you got in those bags?" Leo asked him.

DeVonte set one bag on the floor. "I killed my brother."

Leo finished his beer. "What are you talking about?"

From the other bag, DeVonte withdrew Jinx's severed head and held it up.

Leo was speechless. *The son of a bitch killed my best friend,* he thought.

Then DeVonte pulled a pistol, shot him between the eyes, and Leo thought no more.

Chapter 33

In the moonlit cemetery, Tina raised the bottle. There was only a drink left. She handed the vodka to Kaitlyn. "Go ahead and finish it."

"Are you sure? You don't want the last drink?"

Tina shook her head. "I have more in my bedroom."

Kaitlyn cracked a grin. "You always do." She finished the bottle and tossed it into some weeds.

Tina looked at Victor. "You ready to go home, big guy?"

The Rottweiler rose from the ground, leaving his bone in the grass.

"Should we grab his bone?" Kaitlyn said.

"Nah, that's okay. I keep plenty of rawhide bones in my bedroom, too."

They took off walking, leaving the cemetery and reaching the driveway up to Jinx and Leo's compound.

At the top of the hill, Victor took off running across the front lawn and vanished into some trees.

"Should we wait for him?" Kaitlyn said.

"No, it's okay. He may have seen a rabbit, or something. It's no big deal. He has a doggy door on the other side of the house. Victor comes and goes as he pleases."

On the porch, Tina tried to open the front door, but it was locked. "That's weird. They never lock the door. I don't even know if I have my goddamn key."

Reaching into her pocket, Tina found her housekey. Then she unlocked the door, and they stepped inside.

"Holy fucking shit," Kaitlyn said—which were Tina's sentiments exactly, but she kept her poker face.

Leo sat dead on the sofa; he had been shot once through the head. Jinx's severed head sat upright on the coffee table, but was turned away from them, facing instead DeVonte, who stood naked in front of the television, fucking Roxanne's severed head in the mouth while holding a pistol in his other hand.

DeVonte pointed the gun at Tina when she and Kaitlyn entered the room. "Welcome home, ladies. Glad you could make it. This party's just getting started."

"You don't have to kill us," Tina said. "We just wanna go upstairs and drink some more vodka. You can fuck Roxanne's head all night long for all we care."

DeVonte laughed, still pointing the pistol at Tina. Then he pulled Roxanne's head from his penis and tossed it aside. "I killed your two best friends. So I guess that means I'm gonna have to kill you, too. And your girlfriend."

"Listen," Tina said. "We just wanna go drink some more vodka. I mean . . . yes, it sucks that you killed Leo and Jinx. But what the fuck are we supposed to do about it? We can't bring them back. What do you think we're gonna do? Call the police? It's not our style. We can even help you bury the bodies, if you want us to. It's no big deal. We just wanna go drink some more vodka."

DeVonte cocked his head, as if in contemplation, and then he shook it. "Nah. I'll just kill you both, then figure out which of you two I'm gonna fuck first."

As silent as the hallway from which he came, Victor entered the living room and sprinted toward DeVonte, who had no time to react. In the split second before the attack, Tina had time to notice that the Rottweiler's ears lay flat against his skull and that his lips were pulled back from his teeth.

Then Victor was upon him. DeVonte screamed as the Rottweiler hit him in the chest with both front paws, knocking him to the floor. Then Victor clamped his jaws around DeVonte's crotch and chewed upward. Blood and entrails burst out as the Rottweiler tore him apart above the groin. Working his way up, Victor crushed DeVonte's sternum and shattered his chest cavity. When he reached his head and bit down on his face, Tina heard the crunch as DeVonte's skull collapsed beneath Victor's teeth. DeVonte stopped screaming as chunks of flesh, brain, and skull fragments flew from his ruined head.

Then a telephone rang. Tina looked down and saw that it was Leo's phone ringing on the coffee table. Picking it up, she saw the letters S.F. on its screen. "It's Senator Fox."

Kaitlyn cocked her head. "One of the cannibal politicians?"

"Yes," Tina said. "Leo and Jinx had been waiting for him to call them and tell them to hit the road." She accepted the call and put him on speakerphone. "Hello?"

"Hello. Where's Leo?"

"Leo's dead. And so is Jinx."

"Who the fuck is this?"

"This is Tina. They introduced me to you in D.C. not too long ago. Do you remember?"

"Ah, yes. Tina. Of course I remember you. So, Leo and Jinx are dead?"

"Yes. And here's the deal: you and your friends are gonna be needing some food delivered, and my girlfriend and I both need a job. So how about we step in and fill Leo and Jinx's positions?"

There was a pause. "To bring us the food?"

"Yes."

Another pause, then Senator Fox said, "Where's the bus?"

"The bus is in the barn, behind the house, as we speak."

"So you're at Leo and Jinx's house in L.A. right now?"

"Yes."

"Did you kill Leo and Jinx?"

"No. It's a long story. Maybe I'll tell you later."

"Do you have the keys to the bus?"

She looked at Leo's corpse on the sofa, knowing he kept the keys in his pocket. "Yes, we have the keys to the bus."

"What about the attack dog? Is the attack dog still alive?"

She glanced over at Victor, who continued munching on DeVonte's skull. "Yes. And he's our dog, now. Victor is still alive and doing fine."

"Okay. Do you remember where the warehouse is?"

"Yes. It's in downtown Washington, D.C. I remember exactly where it is."

"Okay. Be here two weeks from today, on the twenty-seventh, at six p.m. Pull the bus around back just like Jinx and Leo did. I'll have some men offload the captives when you get here. And remember: we need variety. We like men, women, *and* children, so keep that in mind when you're filling up the bus."

"Got it," Tina said. "We'll see you in two weeks."

Chapter 34

In Somerset, Kentucky, at Pinecrest Psychiatric Hospital, Linda swiped her name badge and entered the building. In the lobby, one of her favorite patients sat in a wheelchair dropping fish food into an aquarium.

"Hello, Miss Betty," Linda said. "How are you?"

Miss Betty rolled her wheelchair back from the tank and spun around. "I'm bored. Did you bring me something to read?"

Linda withdrew a paperback novel from her purse.

Miss Betty took the book and examined its cover. "Thank you, Linda."

"You're welcome."

At the nurses' station, one of her co-workers told Linda, "Bernice wants to see you in her office."

"Maybe I'm getting a raise."

The woman laughed. "You wish. I think she wants to brief you on the new patient."

"New patient?"

"A dwarf. He's locked in C-Wing right now. I forgot his name, but everyone says he's violent."

Linda crossed the building. The door to the executive director's office was open, but she knocked anyway.

Bernice Dubois looked up from her desk. "Come on in."

Linda entered the office and sat down. "New patient?"

"Yes. Ivan Sawyer. Twenty years old, according to his records, but he looks older. Spent most of his teenage years in juvenile prisons. Once he turned eighteen, he apparently stopped breaking the law. I don't know how long he will be here."

"Are his parents still alive?"

Bernice removed her glasses. "I have no idea."

"And he's a dwarf?"

"Yes. He's on C-Wing. Shall I take you to meet him?"

"No, that's okay. I'll grab some coffee first. But I heard he's violent. Will he try to harm me?"

The director shook her head. "No. He's in a straitjacket."

***

After drinking a cup of coffee, Linda deactivated C-Wing's alarm with a numerical key sequence. Then she opened the door and entered the hall.

All doors on both sides were locked, but the language of the mad was a cacophony of screams and laughter. She hated coming to this part of the facility, and usually deferred the care of these patients to the LPNs under her supervision.

Ivan Sawyer was in the last room on the left. Linda stared at a chart on her clipboard as she strode to his door, then peered through the square window of safety glass.

The dwarf sat on the floor in a corner of the room, banging the back of his bald head against a padded wall.

Linda unlocked the door and entered the room.

The stench of excrement hit her immediately. She covered her nose, but the dwarf did not acknowledge her.

"Ivan?" she said. "Have you had an accident?"

He looked up at her and smiled. His teeth were black. "I've managed to shit my britches, but I'd contest your implication that a bowel movement is an accident." Using his head, he gestured toward the metal toilet in the opposite corner. "I would have been happy to use the commode, but that would be impossible in a straitjacket." He then licked his lips, and winked. "Would you do me a favor and clean my dirty ass?"

Unclipping a pen from her breast pocket, Linda pretended to scribble on her chart. "I'll send someone to clean you and change your clothes."

Ivan smiled again. "Oh, come on. I want you to do it."

Linda returned his smile. "Hold that thought."

She left the room and locked the door behind her.

***

For a week, using his teeth, Ivan tried to unbuckle the harnesses of his straitjacket. Then the straitjacket was removed and he was transferred from his padded cell to a room on B-Wing. After giving him a wheelchair he didn't need, a therapist gave him permission to roam the halls, or to hang out in the dayroom and watch TV.

All of this suited Ivan fine as he plotted his escape.

***

One morning, after clocking in at work, Linda knew something was wrong as soon as she stepped into the dayroom. The attendants wore panic on their faces, and she heard screams coming from the nurses' station. Linda ran toward the noise.

She saw blood on the walls at the junction of B-Wing and C-Wing. Then she saw the executive director lying dead on the floor. Bernice Dubois's throat had been slashed.

The dwarf, Ivan Sawyer, held a baby in his arms and pressed a shard of glass to its neck. The encasement of a fire extinguisher on the wall behind him had been shattered.

"Please!" a young woman screamed. "Please, don't hurt my daughter!"

"The only way she lives," Ivan told her, "is if you get me out of here."

"I will!" the mother shrieked. "I'll take you wherever you want to go! Just don't hurt her! Please!"

The baby wore a hooded pink jumpsuit, and Linda noticed a second child—a girl maybe seven or eight years old—standing next to the mother.

"Let the baby go, Ivan," Linda told him. "I'll take you instead. Just let the baby go, and I'll get you out of here."

The dwarf looked up at her. "I remember you, bitch. You made me sit in my own shit until my ass turned red. I owe you one for that. And fine, you can drive. But this baby, her mother, and the little girl are coming with us."

Ivan made Linda lead the way, then followed her, the mother, and the little girl out to Linda's car.

After Linda got in behind the steering wheel, he made the mother sit up front on the passenger's side. He then climbed into the back next to the little girl with the shard of glass pressed to the baby's neck.

When Linda started the engine, the baby began to cry.

***

An hour later, still in scrubs, Linda continued driving east. She was more concerned about the baby in the back than her own safety. Every time she glanced into the rearview, she saw the dwarf holding the shard to the baby's neck. The baby's sister—*Faith, eight years old,* Linda had learned—sat next to him and didn't say a word.

On the passenger's side, the baby's mother—*Nikki,* Linda had learned—gnawed on her fingernails and wept.

A few miles east, after they crossed from Kentucky into Virginia, the baby started crying again.

"Turn the radio up," Ivan said, "or I'll give this goddamn baby something to cry about."

Linda reached for the volume control, but Nikki beat her to it.

***

Ivan decided that it was time to switch vehicles. They had been in Linda's car for too long, and he considered himself fortunate to have made it to the state of Virginia.

The baby—*Lainey,* he had learned—lay sleeping between him and her sister.

Holding the shard close to Lainey's neck, Ivan told Linda to find the nearest shopping mall.

***

Mary loved shopping for Christmas, and though her favorite holiday was still a few months away, she enjoyed getting started before the frenzy began. Her husband was home with their children, and she lost track of time at the mall.

Finished shopping, Mary left the mall and crossed the parking lot, lugging her purchases to her minivan. Unlocking the van, Mary put her purchases behind its third-row seats.

After closing the rear hatch, she turned and saw a young woman standing before her. The young woman appeared to have been crying.

"Are you okay?" Mary asked her. "Can I help you?"

Then a blow to her head spun her around.

***

Nikki hated what she was doing, what she was being forced to do, but the dwarf—holding the shard of glass to Lainey's throat in Linda's car—had told her to attack the woman with the minivan. And so she had retrieved a metal flashlight from Linda's glove compartment.

The woman did not go down after the first blow. Instead, she just spun sideways, still clutching her purse.

So Nikki struck her again. And again. And again.

She didn't stop until the woman fell bleeding onto the pavement.

***

Ivan got out of the car with the glass shard pressed to the baby's neck.

"Pop the trunk," he told Linda.

She did.

"Now get out of the car," he told her and the little girl. "Both of you."

They did.

Ivan looked around. As far as he could tell, no one had witnessed what was happening.

Then he looked down at the woman on the pavement.

"Put her in the trunk," he told Linda and Nikki. "And then get in the minivan, all three of you. But get her keys first. And hurry."

Linda grabbed the keys, then she and Nikki lifted the woman and crammed her into the trunk.

"Leave the lid open," he told them. "I'll get her money."

The two women left the trunk open and just stood there.

"Now get in the goddamn van," Ivan said. "All three of you. Linda, you're driving. Nikki, you'll ride up front with Linda. Faith, you're riding in the back with me."

Nikki said, "Just be careful with Lainey."

"If you don't get in the van, I'll cut this baby's throat."

Faith got in first, climbing into the minivan's middle row of seats. Then Nikki got in on the passenger's side, and Linda sat down behind the steering wheel.

Ivan swept his gaze across the parking lot. He saw a few people in the distance, but no one paid them any attention.

Holding Lainey with his left arm, he searched the woman's purse, finding some cash and putting it in his pocket. Then he sliced the unconscious woman's throat wide open and closed the trunk.

With the dripping shard pressed to Lainey's neck, Ivan climbed into the minivan's second row of seats. "Time to go, ladies."

Linda started the engine and drove them away.

***

"Ivan," Linda said, tired of driving, "we're almost out of gas." She looked into the rearview mirror and saw that Lainey was asleep.

"Well," Ivan said, "I hope one of you ladies has some gas money, or this little bundle of joy here loses an ear."

On the passenger's seat, Nikki spun around. "I have some cash. Will you please stop talking about hurting her?"

"I will talk," Ivan said, "about whatever I want until I get where I am going."

"Which is *where?*" Linda said. "Where exactly are we taking you?"

"Right now we're just looking for the nearest gas station."

Linda gripped the steering wheel tighter. "I know *that*. I meant . . . never mind."

"Don't worry about it," the dwarf said. "If you get me where I'm going, you'll all be free to go."

Nikki turned around again. "Is that a promise?"

"Yes. You have my word."

***

As Linda drove, she tried to fill her mind with pleasant thoughts. They traveled in silence for a while, heading east on a road somewhere in Virginia.

Eventually, she stopped at an old store with two fuel dispensers in front of the building. She parked by one of the pumps and killed the engine.

"Okay," Ivan said. "I'll stay here with Faith and Lainey. Linda, you pump the gas. Nikki, you go in and pay. And you'd better be cool, too, because if anything seems suspicious—and I'm talking about a cop pulling us over down the road—I'm gonna turn this baby's face into confetti. Do you understand me?"

"Yes," Nikki said. "I understand."

Linda got out first, then Nikki followed suit. Linda filled the tank and got back in. Nikki returned soon thereafter with a plastic bag.

"Did you get some beer?" Ivan asked.

"No, I got us some food. And some applesauce for Lainey."

"Fine," Ivan said. "I'll go in and grab a beer. Be right back." He grabbed Lainey, got out, and carried her toward the store.

"My god," Nikki said. "This can't be happening."

Linda ran fingers through her hair. "Did you tell anyone in the store what's going on?"

"No. I couldn't. You heard him. He'll kill her."

"How many people are in there?"

"Just one. Some old man behind the cash register."

"I'm tired," Linda said. "And I'm getting hungry, too."

Nikki handed her a bag of chips.

***

Charlie Slater had been in business for over fifty years, and in all that time he had seen some strange people enter his store, but when the hideous dwarf walked in holding the baby he was speechless. He had watched the dwarf get out of the minivan, and he therefore knew that the dwarf was with the woman who had just left the store acting funny, so something was amiss, no doubt about it.

As the dwarf grabbed a beer from the beer cooler, the baby started crying.

The dwarf brought the crying baby to the cash register. "How much do you want for this bottle of beer?"

"Take it," Charlie said. "Just take the goddamn thing and get outta here."

***

Ivan could tell the old man didn't like him. Setting his bottle on the floor, he began rocking Lainey back and forth. He then produced the glass shard from his pocket and looked up at the old man. "What would you do if someone tried to rob you?"

"I'd shoot the son of a bitch." The old man pulled a revolver from somewhere beneath the cash register. "I'd shoot the son of a bitch between the eyes."

It was the exact response Ivan had been hoping for, and he pressed the glass shard to Lainey's face. "Here's the deal, mister. You're gonna give me that handgun, along with all the cash in the register, or I'm gonna start cutting this baby's face."

The old man, dipping snuff, spat into his spit cup. "You wouldn't dare."

"Try me."

"Look, just take the goddamn beer and get outta here. I don't know what your story is, and I don't wanna know."

Ivan slashed the baby's face down the middle from her forehead to her mouth. As blood gushed into her eyes, the baby screamed.

"Jesus Christ!" the old man said. "You done went and scarred that baby for life!" He opened the register, took the cash out, and set it on the counter. "Take it! Take it all and get the hell outta here!"

"The gun," Ivan said, as Lainey bled and screamed in his arms. "Put the gun down with the money, or I'll cut this bitch again."

The old man set the gun down next to the money.

Ivan grabbed the gun, aimed it up at the old man's face, and shot him between the eyes. Then he slammed Lainey to the floor and shot her through the head.

Pocketing the money, Ivan rushed out of the store, hiding the gun behind his back, carrying the bottle of beer in his other hand.

When he reached the minivan, Nikki opened the passenger door and got out. "Was that gunfire? Where the hell is Lainey?"

Pointing the gun at Linda (whose hands were on the steering wheel), Ivan told Nikki, "Your daughter's still inside. She's dead."

"No!" Nikki screamed. She took off running toward the store.

Ivan turned, aimed the gun at the back of Nikki's head, and fired once, killing her instantly.

He then climbed in up front—aiming the gun at Linda—and closed the passenger door. "Drive."

"Where to?"

"We'll find out when we get there."

Linda put the van on the road and headed north.

***

He killed her, Linda thought, behind the steering wheel, on a two-lane road headed back to the interstate. *Which means he probably killed the baby, too. Which also means he'll kill me and Faith.*

She already knew that Faith was wearing a seatbelt, but she looked into the rearview to confirm it: yes, like Linda, Faith was wearing a seatbelt.

Then she looked at Ivan and saw that he was not. Instead, he sat with his back against the passenger door, aiming the gun at Linda.

She decided to crash the van.

Maybe he'll drop the gun if I crash the van.

She yanked the steering wheel to the left and slammed the brake pedal, sending the van into a spin. Then it crashed into a tree on the passenger's side. The impact sent Ivan's body crashing into Linda. As she had hoped, the gun fell from his hand and landed on the floorboard between her feet. She picked it up and aimed it at his face.

"Bitch," he said, reaching for the gun.

Linda squeezed the trigger, shooting Ivan through the head. She watched his skull break apart in two directions—saw a wash of blood and brain spray the passenger's-side window.

Then she dropped the gun and turned around. "Are you okay?"

Faith nodded.

"Let's get out of here," Linda said.

They got out.

Linda looked around. For as far as she could see, nothing but trees lined both sides of the road. To the west, the sun was going down. To the east, the first stars of twilight were sparkling.

A car approached them, slowed down, and accelerated away. Moments later, a truck did the same thing.

Then a bus stopped and the passenger's-side window came down. "Are you okay?" a young woman asked them.

"I think so," Linda said. "Can you give us a ride to a police station? Or a hospital?"

"Sure." The woman opened the door. "Come on in."

Leading Faith into the bus, Linda saw another young woman behind the steering wheel. "Thanks so much for stopping," Linda said. "We appreciate it."

The woman on the passenger's side stood up. "What are your names?"

Linda put an arm around the child. "I'm Linda, and this is Faith. We've had an unbelievably bad day."

Faith pointed toward the back. "Why are all those people chained to poles?"

Turning around, Linda saw naked men, women, and children (many of whom were bleeding) chained to poles throughout the bus—and the largest Rottweiler she had ever seen stood watching her in front of all those people.

Linda turned back around. "What the hell is going on here?"

The woman raised a gun. "Your bad day just got worse."

Then she clubbed Linda alongside the head with the gun and knocked her out.

Chapter 35

On the passenger's side, while Tina drove, Kaitlyn admired the historic landmarks of Washington, D.C. that she recognized from television.

Soon thereafter, Tina parked the bus behind a warehouse and killed the engine.

Kaitlyn took a drink of vodka. "This is the place that looks like a ballroom inside?"

Tina nodded. "The front of it does. The back just looks like a warehouse." Then she summoned the Rottweiler, and Victor joined them in the cockpit.

"Simmer," Tina told him.

Victor turned and headed toward the back.

"Simmer?" Kaitlyn said, as one of the garage doors straight ahead rose open.

Tina started the engine. "It takes him off attack status." Then she drove the bus into the warehouse.

Once inside, men in black suits greeted them when they stepped out of the bus. Most of them held either shotguns or machine guns.

Kaitlyn looked around. Beyond the shipping-and-receiving area, through a set of double doors through which servers came and went, she caught glimpses of the red ballroom Tina described. The ballroom was packed with men in white tuxedos and women in white dresses and ball gowns.

Then a man in a black tuxedo approached them, smiling. He set a briefcase on the floor. "Hello, Tina. It's good to see you again. And this must be your friend, Kaitlyn."

"*Girl*friend," Tina corrected.

He nodded at Kaitlyn. "I'm Senator Fox. It's nice to meet you."

"It's nice to meet you, too."

He returned his gaze to Tina. "How many did you bring us?"

"Twelve. We were gonna stop at ten, but then we found two more in Virginia."

"Excellent!"

Tina handed him a key. "This fits all their handcuffs. They're handcuffed to chains attached to the poles."

Senator Fox gave the key to a man with a machine gun. Then he told two men with shotguns to help the man offload the captives.

Kaitlyn watched the three men enter the bus. Soon thereafter, they forced the four male captives—still naked—from the bus into a hallway lined with freezers. From where Kaitlyn stood, each walk-in freezer appeared to be the size of a prison cell.

One by one, the men with shotguns blew the four captives' heads off. Then they put the corpses in separate freezers and closed the doors.

Next, the men forced the five women off the bus. They killed the women, too, and put their bodies in separate freezers, also.

Then they forced the three children off the bus.

"Wait," Senator Fox told them, pointing at Faith. "Take this one back to my room and tie her up. I wanna have a little fun with this one."

As the man with the machine gun dragged her away, the two men with shotguns forced the other two children into the hallway lined with freezers and blew their heads off.

From the floor, Senator Fox picked up the briefcase and handed it to Tina. "Here's your money. Your services will be needed again soon. We'll be in touch."

Kaitlyn followed Tina back into the bus. Tina started the engine and backed the bus out of the warehouse.

In the parking lot, as Tina turned the bus around, Kaitlyn lit a cigarette. "I can't believe it's only ten a.m."

Victor lay behind them, gnawing on a rawhide bone.

"We should go to the beach," Tina said.

"The beach?"

"Yes. You've never seen the Atlantic Ocean, have you?"

Grabbing the bottle of vodka, Kaitlyn took a drink. "Nope. Just the Pacific."

"Virginia Beach is only three hours away. We can stop and get a frisbee for Victor. You wanna go?"

"Let's do it," Kaitlyn said. "I love you."

"I love you, too."

Tina put the bus back on the road.

About the Author

Splatterpunk Award-nominated and Godless Award-winning author Brian Bowyer has been writing stories and music for most of his life. He has lived throughout the United States. He has worked as a janitor, a banker, a bartender, a bouncer, and a bomb maker for a coal-testing laboratory. He currently lives and writes in Ohio. You can contact him at brian.bowyer@hotmail.com.

Printed in Great Britain
by Amazon